She was coming of age tonight.

"King," Tiffany whispered shakily.

"Don't panic," he said quietly. "It's going to be delicious."

She watched his hand move, as if she were paralyzed. His lean fingers traced her collarbone, his eyes lifted to search her quiet, faintly shocked face. Her eyes were enormous. Probably this was all new to her, and perhaps a little frightening, as well.

"You're of age now. It has to happen with someone," he said.

"Then I want it to happen with you," she whispered, her voice trembling, like her body....

Dear Reader,

This month, Silhouette Romance unveils our newest promotion, VIRGIN BRIDES. This series, which celebrates first love, will feature original titles by some of Romance's best-loved stars, starting with perennial favorite Diana Palmer. In *The Princess Bride*, a feisty debutante sets her marriage sights on a hard-bitten, cynical cowboy. At first King Marshall resists, but when he realizes he may lose this innocent beauty—forever—he finds himself doing the unthinkable: proposing.

Stranded together in a secluded cabin, single mom and marked woman Madison Delaney finds comfort—and love—in *In Care of the Sheriff*, this month's FABULOUS FATHERS title, as well as the first book of Susan Meier's new miniseries, TEXAS FAMILY TIES. Donna Clayton's miniseries MOTHER & CHILD also debuts with *The Stand-by Significant Other*. A workaholic businesswoman accepts her teenage daughter's challenge to "get a life," but she quickly discovers that safe—but irresistibly sexy—suitor Ryan Shane is playing havoc with her heart.

In Laura Anthony's compelling new title, *Bride of a Texas Trueblood*, Deannie Hollis would do *anything* to win back her family homestead—even marry the son of her enemy. In Elizabeth Harbison's sassy story, *Two Brothers and a Bride*, diner waitress Joleen Wheeler finds herself falling for the black-sheep brother of her soon-to-be fiancé.... Finally, Martha Shields tells a heartwarming tale about a woman's quest for a haven and the strong, silent rancher who shows her that *Home is Where Hank is*.

In April and May, look for VIRGIN BRIDES titles by Elizabeth August and Annette Broadrick. And enjoy each and every emotional, heartwarming story to be found in a Silhouette Romance.

Regards,

Joan Marlow Golan

Joan Marlow Golan
Senior Editor Silhouette Books

Please address questions and book requests to:
Silhouette Reader Service
U.S.: 3010 Walden Ave., P.O. Box 1325, Buffalo, NY 14269
Canadian: P.O. Box 609, Fort Erie, Ont. L2A 5X3

DIANA PALMER

THE PRINCESS BRIDE

Silhouette

ROMANCE™

Published by Silhouette Books

America's Publisher of Contemporary Romance

For Matt and Elisha

SILHOUETTE BOOKS

ISBN 0-373-19282-7

THE PRINCESS BRIDE

Copyright © 1998 by Diana Palmer

Printed in U.S.A.

Dear Reader,

I was very pleased to be asked to do a book for Silhouette's VIRGIN BRIDES series. I am a hopeless romantic. I love old-fashioned white weddings and the ideals of innocence and purity that go along with them. There is nobility in the idea of saving intimacy for after the wedding, so that the uniting of two people becomes a holy thing, a true union of minds and souls and bodies— a feast of first times.

We live in a world where purity is more often attacked than admired, where instant gratification seems to outweigh idealism. But there will always be people who honor the traditions of the past, who are willing to stand up for what they believe is right, in a world that seems to believe that nothing is ever wrong.

To all the other hopeless romantics out there who love white weddings and who still believe in purity and innocence and marriages that last, and all those other old-fashioned ideas that are so far out of fashion today, I lovingly dedicate this book.

And just for the record, I had a white wedding myself— twenty-five wonderful years ago.

Love,
Diana Palmer

Chapter One

Tiffany saw him in the distance, riding the big black stallion that had already killed one man. She hated the horse, even as she admitted silently how regal it looked with the tall, taciturn man on its back. A killer horse it might be, but it respected Kingman Marshall. Most people around Jacobsville, Texas, did. His family had lived on the Guadalupe River there since the Civil War, on a ranch called Lariat.

It was Spring, and that meant roundup. It was nothing unusual to see the owner of Lariat in the saddle at dawn lending a hand to rope a stray calf or help work the branding. King kept fit with ranch work, and despite the fact that he shared an office and a business partnership with her father in land and cattle, his staff didn't see a lot of him.

This year, they were using helicopters to mass the far-flung cattle, and they had a corral set up on a wide flat stretch of land where they could dip the cattle, check them, cut out the calves for branding and separate them from their mothers. It was physically demanding work, and no job for a tenderfoot. King wouldn't let Tiffany near it, but it wasn't a front row seat at the corral that she wanted. If she could just get his attention away from the milling cattle on the wide, rolling plain that led to the Guadalupe River, if he'd just look her way...

She stood up on a rickety lower rung of the gray wood fence, avoiding the sticky barbed wire, and waved her creamy Stetson at him. She was a picture of young elegance in her tan jodphurs and sexy pink silk blouse and high black boots. She was a debutante. Her father, Harrison Blair, was King's business partner and friend, and if she chased King, her father encouraged her. It would be a marriage made in heaven. That is, if she could find some way to convince King of it. He was elusive and quite abrasively masculine. It might take more than a young lady of almost twenty-one with a sheltered, monied background to land him. But, then, Tiffany had confidence in herself; she was beautiful and intelligent.

Her long black hair hung to her waist in back, and she refused to have it cut. It suited her tall, slender figure and made an elegant frame for her soft oval face and wide green eyes and creamy complexion. She had a sunny smile, and it never faded. Tiffany was always full of fire, burning with a love of life that her father often said had been reflected in her long-dead mother.

"King!" she called, her voice clear, and it carried in the early-morning air.

He looked toward her. Even at the distance, she could see that cold expression in his pale blue eyes, on his lean, hard face with its finely chiseled features. He was a rich man. He worked hard, and he played hard. He had women, Tiffany knew he did, but he was nothing if not discreet. He was a man's man, and he lived like one. There was no playful boy in that tall, fit body. He'd grown up years ago, the boyishness burned out of him by a rich, alcoholic father who demanded blind obedience from the only child of his shallow, runaway wife.

She watched him ride toward her, easy elegance in the saddle. He reined in at the fence, smiling down at her with faint arrogance. He was powerfully built, with long legs and slim hips and broad shoulders. There wasn't an ounce of fat on him, and with his checked red shirt open at the throat, she got fascinating glimpses of bronzed muscle and thick black hair on the expanse of his sexy chest. Jeans emphasized the powerful muscles of his legs, and he had big, elegant hands that hers longed to feel in passion. Not that she was likely to. He treated her like a child most of the time, or at best, a minor irritation.

"You're out early, tidbit," he remarked in a deep, velvety voice with just a hint of Texas drawl. His eyes, under the shade of his wide-brimmed hat, were a pale, grayish blue and piercing as only blue eyes could be.

"I'm going to be twenty-one tomorrow," she said

pertly. "I'm having a big bash to celebrate, and you have to come. Black tie, and don't you dare bring anyone. You're mine, for the whole evening. It's my birthday and on my birthday I want presents—and you're it. My big present."

His dark brows lifted with amused indulgence. "You might have told me sooner that I was going to be a birthday present," he said. "I have to be in Omaha early Saturday."

"You have your own plane," she reminded him. "You can fly."

"I have to sleep sometimes," he murmured.

"I wouldn't touch that line with a ten-foot pole," she drawled, peeking at him behind her long lashes. "Will you come? If you don't, I'll stuff a pillow up my dress and accuse you of being the culprit. And your reputation will be ruined, you'll be driven out of town on a rail, they'll tar and feather you…"

He chuckled softly at the vivid sparkle in her eyes, the radiant smile. "You witch," he accused. "They'd probably give me a medal for getting through your defenses."

She wondered how he knew that, and reasoned that her proud parent had probably told him all about her reputation for coolness with men.

He lit a cigarette, took a long draw from and blew it out with faint impatience. "Little girls and their little whims," he mused. "All right, I'll whirl you around the floor and toast your coming of age, but I won't stay. I can't spare the time."

"You'll work yourself to death," she complained,

and she was solemn now. "You're only thirty-four and you look forty."

"Times are hard, honey," he mused, smiling at the intensity in that glowering young face. "We've had low prices and drought. It's all I can do to keep my financial head above water."

"You could take the occasional break," she advised. "And I don't mean a night on the town. You could get away from it all and just rest."

"They're full up at the Home," he murmured, grinning at her exasperated look. "Honey, I can't afford vacations, not with times so hard. What are you wearing for this coming-of-age party?" he asked to divert her.

"A dream of a dress. White silk, very low in front, with diamanté straps and a white gardenia in my hair." She laughed.

He pursed his lips. He might as well humor her. "That sounds dangerous," he said softly.

"It will be," she promised, teasing him with her eyes. "You might even notice that I've grown up."

He frowned a little. That flirting wasn't new, but it was disturbing lately. He found himself avoiding little Miss Blair, without really understanding why. His body stirred even as he looked at her, and he moved restlessly in the saddle. She was years too young for him, and a virgin to boot, according to her doting, sheltering father. All those years of obsessive parental protection had led to a very immature and unavailable girl. It wouldn't do to let her too close. Not that anyone ever got close to Kingman Marshall, not even his infrequent lovers. He had good reason to keep women at a distance. His upbringing had taught him too well that women were untrustworthy and treacherous.

"What time?" he asked on a resigned note.

"About seven?"

He paused thoughtfully for a minute. "Okay." He tilted his wide-brimmed hat over his eyes. "But only for an hour or so."

"Great!"

He didn't say goodbye. Of course, he never had. He wheeled the stallion and rode off, man and horse so damned arrogant that she felt like flinging something at his tall head. He was delicious, she thought, and her body felt hot all over just looking at him. On the ground he towered over her, lean and hard-muscled and sexy as all hell. She loved watching him.

With a long, unsteady sigh, she finally turned away and remounted her mare. She wondered sometimes why she bothered hero-worshiping such a man. One of these days he'd get married and she'd just die. God forbid that he'd marry anybody but herself!

That was when the first shock of reality hit her squarely between the eyes. Why, she had to ask herself, would a man like that, a mature man with all the worldly advantages, want a young and inexperienced woman like herself at his side? The question worried her so badly that she almost lost control of her mount. She'd never questioned her chances with

King before. She'd never dared. The truth of her situation was unpalatable and a little frightening. She'd never even considered a life without him. What if she had to?

As she rode back toward her own house, on the property that joined King's massive holdings, she noticed the color of the grass. It was like barbed wire in places, very dry and scant. That boded ill for the cattle, and if rain didn't come soon, all that new grass was going to burn up under a hot Texas sun. She knew a lot about the cattle business. After all, her father had owned feedlots since her youth, and she was an only child who worked hard to share his interests. She knew that if there wasn't enough hay by the end of summer, King was going to have to import feed to get his cattle through the winter. The cost of that was prohibitive. It had something to do with black figures going red in the last column, and that could mean disaster for someone with a cow-calf operation the size of King's.

Ah, well, she mused, if King went bust, she supposed that she could get a job and support him. Just the thought of it doubled her over with silvery laughter. King's pride would never permit that sort of help.

Even the Guadalupe was down. She sat on a small rise in the trees, looking at its watery width. The river, like this part of Texas, had a lot of history in it. Archaeologists had found Indian camps on the Guadalupe that dated back seven thousand years,

and because of that, part of it had been designated
a National Historic Shrine.

In more recent history, freight handlers on their
way to San Antonio had crossed the river in DeWitt
County on a ferryboat. In Cuero, a nice drive from
Lariat, was the beginning of the Chisolm Trail. In
nearby Goliad County was the small town of Goliad,
where Texas patriots were slaughtered by the Mexican army back in 1836, just days after the bloodbath
at the Alamo. Looking at the landscape, it was easy
to imagine the first Spanish settlers, the robed priests
founding missions, the Mexican Army with proud,
arrogant Santa Anna at its fore, the Texas patriots
fighting to the last breath, the pioneers and the settlers, the Indians and the immigrants, the cowboys
and cattle barons and desperadoes. Tiffany sighed,
trying to imagine it all.

King, she thought, would have fitted in very well
with the past. Except that he had a blasé attitude
toward life and women, probably a result of having
too much money and time on his hands. Despite his
hard work at roundup, he spent a lot of time in his
office, and on the phone, and also on the road. He
was so geared to making money that he seemed to
have forgotten how to enjoy it. She rode home
slowly, a little depressed because she'd had to work
so hard just to get King to agree to come to her
party. And still haunting her was that unpleasant
speculation about a future without King.

Her father was just on his way out the door when
she walked up from the stables. The house was

stucco, a big sprawling yellow ranch house. It had a small formal garden off the patio, a swimming pool behind, a garage where Tiffany's red Jaguar convertible and her father's gray Mercedes-Benz dwelled, and towering live oak and pecan trees all around. The Guadalupe River was close, but not too close, and Texas stretched like a yellow-green bolt of cloth in all directions to an open, spacious horizon.

"There you are," Harrison Blair muttered. He was tall and gray-headed and green-eyed. Very elegant, despite his slight paunch and his habit of stooping because of a bad back. "I'm late for a board meeting. The caterer called about your party...something about the cheese straws not doing."

"I'll give Lettie a ring. She'll do them for her if I ask her nicely," she promised, grinning as she thought of the elderly lady who was her godmother. "King's coming to my party. I ran him to ground at the river."

He looked over his glasses at her, his heavily lined face vaguely reminiscent of an anorexic bassett hound; not that she'd ever have said anything hurtful to her parent. She adored him. "You make him sound like a fox," he remarked. "Careful, girl, or you'll chase him into a hollow stump and lose him."

"Not me," she laughed, her whole face bright with young certainty. "You just wait. I'll be dangling a diamond one of these days. He can't resist me. He just doesn't know it yet."

He only shook his head. She was so young. She hadn't learned yet that life had a way of giving with one hand, only to take back with the other. Oh, well, she had plenty of years to learn those hard lessons. Let her enjoy it while she could. He knew that King would never settle for a child-woman like his beautiful daughter, but it was something she was going to have to accept one of these days.

"I hope to be back by four," he said, reaching down to peck her affectionately on one cheek. "Are we having champagne? If we are, I hope you told the caterer. I'm not breaking out my private stock until you get married."

"Yes, we are, and yes, I told them," she assured him. "After all, I don't become twenty-one every day."

He studied her with quiet pride. "You look like your mother," he said. "She'd be as proud of you as I am."

She smiled faintly. "Yes." Her mother had been dead a long time, but the memories were bittersweet. The late Mrs. Blair had been vivacious and sparkling, a sapphire in a diamond setting. Her father had never remarried, and seemed not to be inclined toward the company of other women. He'd told Tiffany once that true love was a pretty rare commodity. He and her mother had been so blessed. He was content enough with his memories.

"How many people are we expecting, by the way?" he asked as he put on his Stetson.

"About forty," she said. "Not an overwhelming

number. Just some of my friends and some of King's.'' She grinned. ''I'm making sure they're compatible before I railroad him to the altar.''

He burst out laughing. She was incorrigible and definitely his child, with her keen business sense, he told himself.

''Do you reckon they'll have a lot in common?''

She pursed her pretty lips. ''Money and cattle,'' she reminded him, ''are always a good mix. Besides, King's friends are almost all politicians. They pride themselves on finding things in common with potential voters.''

He winked. ''Good thought.''

She waved and went to call Lettie about doing the cheese straws and the caterers to finalize the arrangements. She was a good hostess, and she enjoyed parties. It was a challenge to find compatible people and put them together in a hospitable atmosphere. So far, she'd done well. Now it was time to show King how organized she was.

The flowers and the caterer had just arrived when she went down the long hall to her room to dress. She was nibbling at a chicken wing on the way up, hoping that she wouldn't starve. There was going to be an hors d'oeuvres table and a drinks bar, but no sit-down dinner. She'd decided that she'd rather dance than eat, and she'd hired a competent local band to play. They were in the ballroom now, tuning up, while Cass, the housekeeper, was watching some of the ranch's lean, faintly disgusted cowboys set up chairs and clear back the furniture. They hated being used as inside labor and their accusing glances let her know it. But she grinned and they melted. Most of them were older hands who'd been with her father since she was a little girl. Like her father, they'd spoiled her, too.

She darted up the staircase, wild with excitement about the evening ahead. King didn't come to the house often, only when her father wanted to talk business away from work, or occasionally for drinks with some of her father's acquaintances. To have him come to a party was new and stimulating. Especially if it ended the way she planned. She had her sights well and truly set on the big rancher. Now she had to take aim.

Chapter Two

Tiffany's evening gown was created by a San Antonio designer, who also happened to own a boutique in one of the larger malls there. Since Jacobsville was halfway between San Antonio and Victoria, it wasn't too long a drive. Tiffany had fallen in love with the gown at first sight. The fact that it had cost every penny of her allowance hadn't even slowed her down. It was simple, sophisticated, and just the thing to make King realize she was a woman. The low-cut bodice left the curve of her full breasts seductively bare and the diamanté straps were hardly any support at all. They looked as if they might give way any second, and that was the charm of the dress. Its silky white length fell softly to just the top of her oyster satin pumps with their rhinestone clips. She put her long hair in an elaborate hairdo, and pinned it with diamond hairpins.

The small silk gardenia in a soft wave was a last-minute addition, and the effect was dynamite. She looked innocently seductive. Just right.

She was a little nervous as she made her way down the curve of the elegant, gray-carpeted staircase. Guests were already arriving, and most of these early ones were around King's age. They were successful businessmen, politicians mostly, with exquisitely dressed wives and girlfriends on their arms. For just an instant, Tiffany felt young and uneasy. And then she pinned on her finishing-school smile and threw herself into the job of hostessing.

She pretended beautifully. No one knew that her slender legs were unsteady. In fact, a friend of one of the younger politicians, a bachelor clerk named Wyatt Corbin, took the smile for an invitation and stuck to her like glue. He was good-looking in a tall, gangly redheaded way, but he wasn't very sophisticated. Even if he had been, Tiffany had her heart set on King, and she darted from group to group, trying to shake her admirer.

Unfortunately he was stubborn. He led her onto the dance floor and into a gay waltz, just as King came into the room.

Tiffany felt like screaming. King looked incredibly handsome in his dark evening clothes. His tuxedo emphasized his dark good looks, and the white of his silk shirt brought out his dark eyes and hair. He spared Tiffany an amused glance and turned to meet the onslaught of two unattached, beautiful older women. His secretary, Carla Stark, hadn't been invited—Tiffany had been resolute about that. There was enough gossip about those two, already, and Carla was unfair competition.

It was the unkindest cut of all, and thanks to this redheaded clown dancing with her, she'd lost her chance. She smiled sweetly at him and suddenly brought down her foot on his toe with perfect accuracy.

"Ouch!" he moaned, sucking in his breath.

"I'm so sorry, Wyatt," Tiffany murmured, batting her eyelashes at him. "Did I step on your poor foot?"

"My fault, I moved the wrong way," he drawled, forcing a smile. "You dance beautifully, Miss Blair."

What a charming liar, she thought. She glanced at King, but he wasn't even looking at her. He was talking and smiling at a devastating blonde, probably a politician's daughter, who looked as if she'd just discovered the best present of all under a Christmas tree. No thanks to me, Tiffany thought miserably.

Well, two could play at ignoring, she thought, and turned the full effect of her green eyes on Wyatt. Well, happy birthday to me, she thought silently, and asked him about his job. It was assistant city clerk or some such thing, and he held forth about his duties for the rest of the waltz, and the one that followed.

King had moved to the sofa with the vivacious little blonde, where he looked as if he might set up housekeeping. Tiffany wanted to throw back her head and scream with outrage. Whose party was this, anyway, and which politician was that little blonde with? She began scanning the room for unattached older men.

"I guess I ought to dance with Becky, at least once," Wyatt sighed after a minute. "She's my cousin. I didn't have anyone else to bring. Excuse me a second, will you?"

He left her and went straight toward the blonde who was dominating King. But if he expected the blonde to sacrifice that prize, he was sadly mistaken. They spoke in whispers, while King glanced past Wyatt at Tiffany with a mocking, worldly look. She turned her back and went to the punch bowl.

Wyatt was back in a minute. "She doesn't mind being deserted," he chuckled. "She's found a cattle baron to try her wiles on. That's Kingman Marshall over there, you know."

Tiffany looked at him blankly. "Oh, is it?" she asked innocently, and tried not to show how furious she really was. Between Wyatt and his cousin, they'd ruined her birthday party.

"I wonder why he's here?" he frowned.

She caught his hand. "Let's dance," she muttered, and dragged him back onto the dance floor.

For the rest of the evening, she monopolized Wyatt, ignoring King as pointedly as if she'd never seen him before and never cared to again. Let him flirt with other women at her party. Let him break her heart. He was never going to know it. She'd hold her chin up if it killed her. She smiled at Wyatt and flirted outrageously, the very life and soul of her party, right up to the minute when she cut the cake and asked Wyatt to help her serve it. King didn't seem to notice or care that she ignored him. But her father was puzzled, staring at her incomprehensibly.

"This party is so boring," Tiffany said an hour later, when she felt she couldn't take another single minute of the blonde clinging to King on the dance floor. "Let's go for a ride."

Wyatt looked uncomfortable. "Well...I came in a truck," he began.

"We'll take my Jag."

"You've got a Jaguar?"

She didn't need to say another word. Without even a glance in King's direction, she waved at her father and blew him a kiss, dragging Wyatt along behind her toward the front door. Not that he needed much coaxing. He seemed overwhelmed when she tossed him the keys and climbed into the passenger seat of the sleek red car.

"You mean, I can drive this?" he burst out.

"Sure. Go ahead. It's insured. But I like to go fast, Wyatt," she said. And for tonight, that was true. She was sick of the party, sick of King, sick of her life. She hurt in ways she'd never realized she could. She only wanted to get away, to escape.

He started the car and stood down on the accelerator. Tiffany had her window down, letting the breeze whip through her hair. She deliberately pulled out the diamond hairpins and tucked them into her purse, letting her long, black hair free and fly on the wind. The champagne she'd had to drink was beginning to take effect and was making her feel very good indeed. The speed of the elegant little car added to her false euphoria. Why, she didn't care about King's indifference. She didn't care at all!

"What a car!" Wyatt breathed, wheeling it out onto the main road.

"Isn't it, though?" she laughed. She leaned back and closed her eyes. She wouldn't think about King. "Go faster, Wyatt, we're positively crawling! I love speed, don't you?"

Of course he did. And he didn't need a second prompting. He put the accelerator peddle to the floor, and twelve cylinders jumped into play as the elegant vehicle shot forward like its sleek and dangerous namesake.

She laughed, silvery bells in the darkness, enjoying the unbridled speed, the fury of motion. Yes, this would blow away all the cobwebs, all the hurt, this would...!

The sound of sirens behind them brought her to her senses. She glanced over the seat and saw blue bubbles spinning around, atop a police car.

"Oh, for heaven's sake, where did he come from!" she gasped. "I never saw the car. They must parachute down from treetops," she muttered, and then giggled at her own remark.

Wyatt slowed the car and pulled onto the shoulder, his face rapidly becoming the color of his hair.

He glanced at Tiffany. "Gosh, I'm sorry. And on your birthday, too!"

"I don't care. I told you to do it," she reminded him.

A tall policeman came to the side of the car and watched Wyatt fumble to power the window down.

"Good God. *Wyatt?*" the officer gasped.

"That's right, Bill," Wyatt sighed, producing his driver's license. "Tiffany Blair, this is Bill Harris. He's one of our newest local policemen and a cousin of mine."

"Nice to meet you, officer—although I wish it was under better circumstances," Tiffany said with a weak smile. "I should get the ticket, not Wyatt. It's my car, and I asked him to go faster."

"I clocked you at eighty-five, you know," he told Wyatt gently. "I sure do hate to do this, Wyatt. Mr. Clark is going to be pretty sore at you. He just had a mouthful to say about speeders."

"The mayor hates me anyway," Wyatt groaned.

"I won't tell him you got a ticket if you don't." Bill grinned.

"Want to bet he'll find out anyway? Just wait."

"It's all my fault," Tiffany muttered. "And it's my birthday…!"

A sleek, new black European sports car slid in behind the police car and came to a smooth, instant stop. A minute later, King got out and came along to join the small group.

"What's the trouble, Bill?" he asked the policeman.

"They were speeding, Mr. Marshall," the officer said. "I'll have to give him a ticket. He was mortally flying."

"I can guess why," King mused, staring past Wyatt at a pale Tiffany.

"Nobody held a gun on me," Wyatt said gently. "It's my own fault. I could have refused."

"The first lesson of responsibility," King agreed. "Learning to say no. Come on, Tiffany. You've caused enough trouble for one night. I'll drop you off on my way out."

"I won't go one step with you, King...!" she began furiously.

He went around to the passenger side of the Jag, opened the door, and tugged her out. His lean, steely fingers on her bare arm raised chills of excitement where they touched. "I don't have time to argue. You've managed to get Wyatt in enough trouble." He turned to Wyatt. "If you'll bring the Jag back, I think your cousin is ready to leave. Sorry to spoil your evening."

"It wasn't spoiled at all, Mr. Marshall," Wyatt said with a smile at Tiffany. "Except for the speeding ticket, I enjoyed every minute of it!"

"I did, too, Wyatt," Tiffany said. "I...King, will you stop dragging me?"

"No. Good night, Wyatt. Bill."

A chorus of good-nights broke the silence as King led an unwilling, sullen Tiffany back to his own leather-trimmed sports car. He helped her inside, got in under the wheel and started the powerful engine.

"I hate you, King," she ground out as he pulled onto the highway.

"Which is no reason at all for making a criminal of Wyatt."

She glared at him hotly through the darkness. "I did not make him a criminal! I only offered to let him drive the Jaguar."

"And told him how fast to go?"

"He wasn't complaining!"

He glanced sideways at her. Despite the rigid set of her body, and the temper on that lovely face, she excited him. One diamanté strap was halfway down a silky smooth arm, revealing more than a little of a tip-tilted breast. The silk fabric outlined every curve of her body, and he could smell the floral perfume that wafted around her like a seductive cloud. She put his teeth on edge, and it irritated him beyond all reason.

He lit a cigarette that he didn't even want, and abruptly put it out, remembering belatedly that he'd quit smoking just last week. And he was driving faster than he normally did. "I don't know why in hell you invited me over here," he said curtly, "if you planned to spend the whole evening with the damned city clerk."

"Assistant city clerk," she mumbled. She darted a glance at him and pressed a strand of long hair away from her mouth. He looked irritated. His face was harder than usual, and he was driving just as fast as Wyatt had been.

"Whatever the hell he is."

"I didn't realize you'd even noticed what I was doing, King," she replied sweetly, "what with Wyatt's pretty little cousin wrapped around you like a ribbon."

His eyebrows arched. "Wrapped around me?"

"Wasn't she?" she asked, averting her face. "Sorry. It seemed like it to me."

He pulled the car onto the side of the road and turned toward her, letting the engine idle. The hand holding the steering wheel clenched, but his dark eyes were steady on hers; she could see them in the light from the instrument panel.

"Were you jealous, honey?" he taunted, in a tone she'd never heard him use. It was deep and smooth and low-pitched. It made her young body tingle in the oddest way.

"I thought you were supposed to be my guest, that's all," she faltered.

"That's what I thought, too, until you started vamping Wyatt whats-his-name."

His finger toyed with the diamanté strap that had fallen onto her arm. She reached to tug it up, but his lean, hard fingers were suddenly there, preventing her.

Her eyes levered up to meet his quizzically, and in the silence of the car, she could hear her own heartbeat, like a faint drum.

The lean forefinger traced the strap from back to front, softly brushing skin that had never known a man's touch before. She stiffened a little, to feel it so lightly tracing the slope of her breast.

"They...they'll miss us," she said in a voice that sounded wildly high-pitched and frightened.

"Think so?"

He smiled slowly, because he was exciting her, and he liked it. He could see her breasts rising and falling with quick, jerky breaths. He could see her nipples peaking under that silky soft fabric. The pulse in her throat was quick, too, throbbing. She was coming-of-age tonight, in more ways than one.

He reached beside him and slowly, blatantly, turned off the engine before he turned back to Tiffany. There was a full moon, and the light of it and the subdued light of the instrument panel gave him all the illumination he needed.

"King," she whispered shakily.

"Don't panic," he said quietly. "It's going to be delicious."

She watched his hand move, as if she were paralyzed. It drew the strap even further off her arm, slowly, relentlessly, tugging until that side of her silky bodice fell to the hard tip of her nipple. And then he gave it a whisper of a push and it fell completely away, baring her pretty pink breast to eyes that had seen more than their share of women. But this was different. This was Tiffany, who was virginal and young and completely without experience.

That knowledge hardened his body. His lean fingers traced her collarbone, his eyes lifted to search her quiet, faintly shocked face. Her eyes were enormous. Probably this was all new to her, and perhaps a little frightening as well.

"You're of age, now. It has to happen with some-one," he said.

"Then...I want it to happen...with you," she whispered, her voice trembling, like her body.

His pulse jumped. His eyes darkened, glittered. "Do you? I wonder if you realize what you're get-ting into," he murmured. He bent toward her, no-ticing her sudden tension, her wide-eyed apprehen-sion. He checked the slow movement, for an instant; long enough to whisper, "I won't hurt you."

She leaned back against the leather seat as he turned toward her, her body tautening, trembling a little. But it wasn't fear that motivated her. As she met his smoldering eyes, she slowly arched her back, to let the rest of the bodice fall, and saw the male desire in his dark eyes as they looked down at what the movement had uncovered.

"Your breasts are exquisite," he said absently, that tracing hand moving slowly, tenderly, down one tip-tilted slope, making her shudder. "Perfect."

"They ache," she whispered on a sob, her eyes half closed, in thrall to some physical paralysis that made her throb all over with exquisite sensations.

"I can do something about that," he mused with a brief smile.

His forefinger found the very tip of one small breast and traced around it gently, watching it go even harder, feeling it shudder with the tiny consum-mation. He heard the faint gasp break from her lips and looked up at her face, at her wide, misty eyes.

"Yes," he said, as if her expression told him everything. And it did. She wanted him. She'd let him do anything he wanted to do, and he felt hot all over.

She moved against the seat, her body in helpless control now, begging for something, for more than this. Her head went back, her full lips parting, hungry.

He slid his arm under her neck, bringing her body closer to his, his mouth poised just above hers. He watched her as his hand moved, and his lean fingers slowly closed over her breast, taking its soft weight and teasing the nipple with his thumb.

She cried softly at the unexpected pleasure, and bit her lower lip in helpless agony.

"Don't do that," he whispered, bending. "Let me…"

His hard lips touched hers, biting softly at them, tracing them warmly from one side to the other. His nose nuzzled against hers, relaxing her, gentling her, while his hand toyed softly with her breast. "Open your mouth, baby," he breathed as his head lowered again, and he met her open mouth with his.

She moaned harshly at the wild excitement he was arousing in her. She'd never dreamed that a kiss could be so intimate, so sweetly exciting. His tongue pushed past her startled lips, into the soft darkness of her mouth, teasing hers in a silence broken only by the sounds of breathing, and cloth against cloth.

"King," she breathed under his lips. Her hands bit into his hair, his nape, tugging. "Hard, King," she whispered shakily, "hard, hard…!"

He hadn't expected that flash of ardor. It caused

him to be far rougher than he meant to. He crushed her mouth under his, the force of it bending her head back against his shoulder. His searching hand found first one breast, then the other, savoring the warm silk of their contours, the hard tips that told him how aroused she was.

He forgot her age and the time and the place, and suddenly jerked her across him, his hands easing her into the crook of his arm as he bent his head to her body.

"Sweet," he whispered harshly, opening his mouth on her breast. "God, you're sweet...!"

She cried out from the shock of pleasure his mouth gave her, a piercing little sound that excited him even more, and her body arched up toward him like a silky pink sacrifice. Her hands tangled in his thick black hair, holding him there, tears of mingled frustration and sweet anguish trailing down her hot cheeks as the newness of passion racked her.

"Don't...stop," she whimpered, her hands contracting at his nape, pulling him back to her. "Please!"

"I wonder if I could," he murmured with faint self-contempt as he gave in to the exquisite pleasure of tasting her soft skin. "You taste of gardenia petals, except right...here," he whispered as his lips suddenly tugged at a hard nipple, working down until he took her silky breast into his mouth in a warm, soft suction that made her moan endlessly.

His steely fingers bit into her side as he moved the dress further down and shifted her, letting his mouth press warmly against soft skin, tracing her stomach into the soft elastic of her briefs, tracing the briefs to her hips and waist and then back up to the trembling softness of her breasts.

She found the buttons of his jacket, his silk shirt, and fumbled at them, whimpering as she struggled to make them come apart. She wanted to touch him, experience him as he was experiencing her. Without a clue as to what he might want, she tugged at the edges until he moved her hand aside and moved the fabric away for her. She flattened her palm against thick hair and pure man, caressing him with aching pleasure.

"Here," he whispered roughly, moving her so that her soft breasts were crushed against the abrasive warmth of his chest.

He wrapped her up tight, then, moving her against his hair-roughened skin in a delirium of passion, savoring the feel of her breasts, the silkiness of her skin against him. His body was demanding satisfaction, now, hard with urgent need. His hand slid down her back to her spine and he turned her just a little so that he could press her soft hips into his, and let her know how desperately he wanted her.

She gasped as she felt him in passion, felt and understood the changed contours of his body. Her face buried itself in his hot throat and she trembled all over.

"Are you shocked, Tiffany?" he whispered at her ear, his voice a little rough as if he weren't quite in control. "Didn't you know that a man's body grows hard with desire?"

She shivered a little as he moved her blatantly against him, but it didn't shock her. It delighted her. "It's wicked, isn't it, to do this together?" she whispered shakily. Her eyes closed. "But no, I'm not shocked. I want you, too. I want…to be with you. I want to know how it feels to have you…"

He heard the words with mingled joy and shock. His whirling mind began to function again. *Want. Desire. Sex.* His eyes flew open. She was only twenty-one, for God's sake! And a virgin. His business partner's daughter. What the hell was he doing?

He jerked away from her, his eyes going helplessly to her swollen, taut breasts before he managed to pull her arms from around his neck and push her back in her seat. He struggled to get out of the car, his own aching body fighting him as he tried to remove himself from unbearable temptation in time.

He stood by the front fender, his shirt open, his chest damp and throbbing, his body hurting. He bent over a little, letting the wind get to his hot skin. He must be out of his mind!

Tiffany, just coming to her own senses, watched him with eyes that didn't quite register what was going on. And then she knew. It had almost gone too far. He'd started to make love to her, and then he'd remembered who they were and he'd stopped. He must be hurting like the very devil.

She wanted to get out of the car and go to him, but that would probably make things even worse.

She looked down and realized that she was nude to the hips. And he'd seen her like that, touched her...

She tugged her dress back up in a sudden flurry of embarrassment. It had seemed so natural at the time, but now it was shameful. She felt for the straps and pulled the bodice up, keeping her eyes away from her hard, swollen nipples. King had suckled them...

She shuddered with the memory, with new knowledge of him. He'd hate her now, she thought miserably. He'd hate her for letting him go so far, for teasing him. There were names for girls who did that. But she hadn't pulled away, or said no, she recalled. He'd been the one to call a halt, because she couldn't.

Her face went scarlet. She smoothed back her disheveled hair with hands that trembled. How could she face her guests now, like this? Everyone would know what had happened. And what if Wyatt should come along in the Jaguar...?

She looked behind them, but there was no car in sight. And then she realized that they were on King's property, not hers. Had he planned this?

After another minute, she saw him straighten and run a hand through his sweaty hair. He rebuttoned his shirt and tucked it back into his trousers. He did the same with his evening jacket and straightened his tie.

When he finally turned back to get into the car, he looked pale and unapproachable. Tiffany glanced at him as he climbed back in and closed the door, wondering what to say.

"I'll drive you home," he said tersely. "Fasten your seat belt," he added, because she didn't seem to have enough presence of mind to think of it herself.

He started the car without looking at her and turned it around. Minutes later, they were well on the way to her father's house.

It was ablaze with lights, although most of the cars had gone. She looked and saw the Jaguar sitting near the front door. So Wyatt was back. She didn't know what kind of car he was driving, so she couldn't tell if he'd gone or not. She hoped he had, and his cousin with him. She didn't want to see them again.

King pulled up at the front door and stopped, but he didn't cut the engine.

She reached for the door handle and then looked back at him, her face stiff and nervous.

"Are you angry?" she asked softly.

He stared straight ahead. "I don't know."

She nibbled her lower lip, and tasted him there. "I'm not sorry," she said doggedly, her face suddenly full of bravado.

He turned then, his eyes faintly amused. "No. I'm not sorry, either."

She managed a faint smile, despite her embarrassment. "You said it had to happen eventually."

"And you wanted it to happen with me. So you said."

"I meant it," she replied quietly. Her eyes searched his, but she didn't find any secrets there. "I'm not ashamed."

His dark eyes trailed down her body. "You're exquisite, little Tiffany," he said. "But years too young for an affair, and despite tonight's showing, I don't seduce virgins."

"Is an affair all you have to offer?" she asked with new maturity.

He pursed his lips, considering that. "Yes, I think it is. I'm thirty-four. I like my freedom. I don't want the commitment of a wife. Not yet, at least. And you're not old enough for that kind of responsibility. You need a few years to grow up."

She was grown up, but she wasn't going to argue the point with him. Her green eyes twinkled. "Not in bed, I don't."

He took a deep breath. "Tiffany, there's more to a relationship than sex. About which," he added shortly, "you know precious little."

"I can learn," she murmured.

"Damned fast, judging by tonight," he agreed with a wicked smile. "But physical pleasure gets old quickly."

"Between you and me?" she asked, her eyes adoring him. "I don't really think it ever would. I can imagine seducing you in all sorts of unlikely places."

His heart jumped. He shouldn't ask. He shouldn't... "Such as?" he asked in spite of himself.

"Sitting up," she breathed daringly. "In the front seat of a really elegant European sports car parked right in front of my house…"

His blood was beating in his temple. She made him go hot all over with those sultry eyes, that expression…

"You'd better go inside," he said tersely.

"Yes, I suppose I had," she murmured dryly. "It really wouldn't do, would it, what with the risk of someone coming along and seeing us."

It got worse by the second. He was beginning to hurt. "Tiffany…"

She opened the door and glanced back at his hard, set face. He was very dark, and she loved the way he looked in evening clothes. Although now, she'd remember him with his shirt undone and her hands against that sexy, muscular chest.

"Run while you can, cattle baron," she said softly. "I'll be two steps behind."

"I'm an old fox, honey," he returned. "And not easy game."

"We'll see about that," she said, smiling at him. "Good night, lover."

He caught his breath, watching her close the door and blow him a kiss. He had to get away, to think. The last thing he wanted was to find himself on the receiving end of a shotgun wedding. Tiffany was all too tempting, and the best way to handle this was to get away from her for a few weeks, until they both cooled off. A man had to keep a level head, in business and in personal relationships.

He put the car in gear and drove off. Yes, that was what he should do. He'd find himself a nice business trip. Tiffany would get over him. And he'd certainly get over her. He'd had women. He'd known this raging hunger before. But he couldn't satisfy it with a virgin.

He thought about her, the way she'd let him see her, and the aching started all over again. His face hardened as he stepped down on the accelerator. Maybe a long trip would erase that image. Something had to!

Tiffany went back into the house, breathless and worried that her new experiences would show. But they didn't seem to. Wyatt came and asked where she and King had been and she made some light, outrageous reply.

For the rest of the evening, she was the belle of her own ball. But deep inside she was worried about the future. King wasn't going to give in without a fight. She hoped she had what it took to land that big Texas fish. She wanted him more than anything in the whole world. And she wasn't a girl who was used to disappointments.

Chapter Three

"Well, King's left the country," Harrison Blair murmured dryly three days after Tiffany's party. "You don't seem a bit surprised."

"He's running scared," she said pertly, grinning up at her father from the neat crochet stitches she was using to make an afghan for her room. "I don't blame him. If I were a man being pursued by some persistent woman, I'm sure that I'd run, too."

He shook his head. "I'm afraid he isn't running from you," he mused. "He took his secretary with him."

Her heart jumped, but she didn't miss a stitch. "Did he? I hope Carla enjoys the trip. Where did they go?"

"To Nassau. King's talking beef exports with the minister of trade. But I'm sure Carla took a bathing suit along."

She put in three more stitches. Carla Stark was a redhead, very pretty and very eligible and certainly no virgin. She wanted to throw her head back and scream, but that would be juvenile. It was a temporary setback, that was all.

"Nothing to say?" her father asked.

She shrugged. "Nothing to say."

He hesitated. "I don't want to be cruel," he began. "I know you've set your heart on King. But he's thirty-four, sweethcart. You're a very young twenty-one. Maturity takes time. And I've been just a tad overprotective about you. Maybe I was wrong to be so strict about young men."

"It wouldn't really have mattered," she replied ruefully. "It was King from the time I was fourteen. I couldn't even get interested in boys my own age."

"I see."

She put the crochet hook through the ball of yarn and moved it, along with the partially finished afghan, to her work basket. She stood up, pausing long enough to kiss her father's tanned cheek. "Don't worry about me. You might not think so, but I'm tough."

"I don't want you to wear your heart out on King."

She smiled at him. "I won't!"

"Tiff, he's not a marrying man," he said flatly. "And modern attitudes or no, if he seduces you, he's history. He's not playing fast and loose with you."

"He already told me that himself," she assured

him. "He doesn't have any illusions about me, and he said that he's not having an affair with me."

He was taken aback. "He did?"

She nodded. "Of course, he also said he didn't want a wife. But all relationships have these little minor setbacks. And no man really wants to get married, right?"

His face went dark. "Now listen here, you can't seduce him, either!"

"I can if I want to," she replied. "But I won't, so stop looking like a thundercloud. I want a home of my own and children, not a few months of happiness followed by a diamond bracelet and a bouquet of roses."

"Have I missed something here?"

"Lettie said that's how King kisses off his women," she explained. "With a diamond bracelet and a bouquet of roses. Not that any of them last longer than a couple of months," she added with a rueful smile. "Kind of them, isn't it, to let him practice on them until he's ready to marry me?"

His eyes bulged. "What ever happened to the double standard?"

"I told you, I don't want anybody else. I couldn't really expect him to live a life of total abstinence when he didn't know he was going to marry me one day. I mean, he was looking for the perfect woman all this time, and here I was right under his nose. Now that he's aware of me, I'm sure there won't be anybody else. Not even Carla."

Harrison cleared his throat. "Now, Tiffany..."

She grinned. "I hope you want lots of grandchildren. I think kids are just the greatest things in the world!"

"Tiffany…"

"I want a nice cup of tea. How about you?"

"Oolong?"

She grimaced. "Green. I ran out of oolong and forgot to ask Mary to put it on the grocery list this week."

"Green's fine, then, I guess."

"Better than coffee," she teased, and made a face. "I won't be a minute."

He watched her dart off to the kitchen, a pretty picture in jeans and a blue T-shirt, with her long hair in a neat ponytail. She didn't look old enough to date, much less marry.

She was starry-eyed, thinking of a home and children and hardly considering the reality of life with a man like King. He wouldn't want children straight off the bat, even if she thought she did. She was far too young for instant responsibility. Besides that, King wouldn't be happy with an impulsive child who wasn't mature enough to handle business luncheons and the loneliness of a home where King spent time only infrequently. Tiffany would expect constant love and attention, and King couldn't give her that. He sighed, thinking that he was going to go gray-headed worrying about his only child's upcoming broken heart. There seemed no way to avoid it, no way at all.

* * *

Tiffany wasn't thinking about business lunches or having King home only once in a blue moon. She was weaving dreams of little boys and girls playing around her skirts on summer days, and King holding hands with her while they watched television at night. Over and above that, she was plotting how to bring about his downfall. First things first, she considered, and now that she'd caught his eye, she had to keep it focused on herself.

She phoned his office to find out when he was coming back, and wrangled the information that he had a meeting with her father the following Monday just before lunch about a stock transfer.

She spent the weekend planning every move of her campaign. She was going to land that sexy fighting fish, one way or another.

She found an excuse to go into Jacobsville on Monday morning, having spent her entire allowance on a new sultry jade silk dress that clung to her slender curves as if it were a second skin. Her hair was put up neatly in an intricate hairdo, with a jade clip holding a wave in place. With black high heels and a matching bag, she looked elegant and expensive and frankly seductive as she walked into her father's office just as he and King were coming out the door on their way to lunch.

"Tiffany," her father exclaimed, his eyes widening at the sight of her. He'd never seen her appear quite so poised and elegant.

King was doing his share of looking, as well. His

dark eyebrows dove together over glittering pale eyes and his head moved just a fraction to the side as his gaze went over her like seeking hands.

"I don't have a penny left for lunch," she told her father on a pitiful breath. "I spent everything in my purse on this new dress. Do you like it?" She turned around, her body exquisitely posed for King's benefit. His jaw clenched and she had to repress a wicked smile.

"It's very nice, sweetheart," Harrison agreed. "But why can't you use your credit card for lunch?"

"Because I'm going to get some things for an impromptu picnic," she replied. Her eyes lowered demurely.

"You could come to lunch with us," Harrison began.

King looked hunted.

Tiffany saw his expression and smiled gently. "That's sweet of you, Dad, but I really haven't time. Actually, I'm meeting someone. I hope he likes the dress," she added, lowering her head demurely. She was lying her head off, but they didn't know it. "Can I have a ten-dollar bill, please?"

Harrison swept out his wallet. "Take two," he said, handing them to her. He glared at her. "It isn't Wyatt, I hope," he muttered. "He's too easily led."

"No. It's not Wyatt. Thanks, Dad. See you, King."

"Who is it?"

King's deep, half-angry voice stopped her at the

doorway. She turned, her eyebrows lifted as if he'd shocked her with the question. "Nobody you know," she said honestly. "I'll be in by bedtime, Dad."

"How can you go on a picnic in that dress?" King asked shortly.

She smoothed her hand down one shapely hip. "It's not *that* sort of picnic," she murmured demurely. "We're going to have it on the carpet in his living room. He has gas logs in his fireplace. It's going to be so romantic!"

"It's May," King ground out. "Too hot for fires in the fireplace."

"We won't sit too close to it," she said. "Ta, ta."

She went out the door and dived into the elevator, barely able to contain her glee. She'd shaken King. Let him stew over that lie for the rest of the day, she told herself, and maybe he'd feel as uncomfortable as she'd felt when he took his secretary to Nassau!

Of course there was no picnic, because she wasn't meeting anyone. She stopped by a fish and chips place and got a small order and took it home with her. An hour later, she was sprawled in front of her own fireplace, unlit, with a trendy fashion magazine. Lying on her belly on the thick beige carpet, in tight-fitting designer jeans and a low-cut tank top, barefoot and with her long hair loose, she looked the picture of youth.

King's sudden appearance in the doorway shocked her. She hadn't expected to be found out, certainly not so quickly.

"Where is he?" he asked, his hands in his slacks pocket. He glanced around the spacious room. "Hiding under the sofa? Behind a chair?"

She was frozen in position with a small piece of fish in her hand as she gaped at him.

"What a tangled web we weave," he mused.

"I wasn't deceiving you. Well, maybe a little," she acknowledged. Her eyes glared up at him. "You took Carla to Nassau, didn't you? I hope you had fun."

"Like hell you do."

He closed the door behind him abruptly and moved toward her, resplendent in a gray suit, his black hair catching the light from the ceiling and glowing with faint blue lights.

She rolled over and started to get up, but before she could move another inch, he straddled her prone figure and with a movement so smooth that it disconcerted her, he was suddenly full-length over her body on the carpet, balancing only on his forearms.

"I suppose you'll taste of fish," he muttered as he bent and his hard mouth fastened roughly on her lips.

She gasped. His hips shifted violently, his long legs insistent as they parted her thighs and moved quickly between them. His hands trapped her wrists, stilling her faint instinctive protest at the shocking intimacy of his position.

He lifted his mouth a breath away and looked straight into her eyes. One lean leg moved, just briefly, and he pushed forward against her, his body suddenly rigid. He let her feel him swell with desire, and something wickedly masculine flared in his pale, glittering eyes as new sensations registered on her flushed face.

"Now you know how it happens," he murmured, dropping his gaze to her soft, swollen mouth. "And how it feels when it happens. Draw your legs up a little. I want you to feel me completely against you there."

"King!"

He shifted insistently, making her obey him. She felt the intimacy of his hold and gasped, shivering a little at the power and strength of him against her so intimately.

"Pity, that you don't have anybody to compare me with," he mused deeply as his head bent. "But that might be a good thing. I wouldn't want to frighten you…"

His mouth twisted, parting her lips. It was so different from the night of her party. Then, she'd been the aggressor, teasing and tempting him. Now, she was very much on the defensive. He was aroused and insistent and she felt young and uncertain, especially when he began to move in a very seductive way that made her whole body tingle and clench with sensual pleasure.

He heard the little gasp that escaped the lips under his hard mouth, and his head lifted.

He searched her eyes, reading very accurately her response to him. "Didn't you know that pleasure comes of such intimacy?" he whispered.

"Only from...books," she confessed breathlessly. She shivered as he moved again, just enough to make her totally aware of her body's feverish response to that intimate pressure.

"Isn't this more exciting than reading about it?" he teased. His mouth nibbled at her lips. "Open them," he whispered. "Deep kisses are part of the process."

"King, I'm not...not...sure..."

"You're sure," he whispered into her mouth. "You're just apprehensive, and that's natural. They told you it was going to hurt, didn't they?"

She swallowed, aware of dizziness that seemed to possess her.

His teeth nibbled sensually at her lower lip. "I'll give you all the time you need, when it happens," he murmured lazily. "If I can arouse you enough, you won't mind if I hurt you a little. It might even intensify the pleasure."

"I don't understand."

His open mouth brushed over hers. "I know," he murmured. "That's what excites me so. Slide your hands up the back of my thighs and hold me against you."

"Wh...what?"

His mouth began to move between her lips. "You wore that dress to excite me. All right. I'm excited. Now satisfy me."

"I...but I...can't..." she gasped. "King!"

His hands were under her, intimate, touching her in shocking ways.

"Isn't this what you wanted? It's what you implied when you struck that seductive pose and invited me to ravish you right there on the floor of your father's office."

"I did not!"

His thumbs pressed against her in a viciously arousing way, so that when he pushed down with his hips, she lifted to meet them, groaning harshly at the shock of delight that was only the tip of some mysterious iceberg of ecstasy.

"Tell me that again," he challenged.

She couldn't. She was burning up, dying, in anguish. A stranger's hands fought her tank top and the tiny bra under it, pushing them out of the way only seconds before those same hands tugged at his shirt and managed to get under it, against warm muscle and hair.

While he kissed her, she writhed under him, shivering when she felt his skin against her own. Delirious with fevered need, she slid her hands down his flat belly and even as he dragged his mouth from hers to protest, they pressed, trembling, against the swollen length of him through the soft fabric.

He moaned something, shuddered. He rolled abruptly onto his side and drew her hand back to him, moving it softly on his body, teaching her the sensual rhythm he needed.

"Dear God," he whispered, kissing her hungrily.

"No, baby, don't stop," he groaned when her movements slowed. "Touch me. Yes. Yes. Oh, God, yes!"

It was fascinating to see how he reacted to her. Encouraged, she moved closer and her mouth pressed softly, sensually, against the thick hair that covered his chest. He was shaking now. His body was strangely vulnerable, and the knowledge inhibited her.

He rolled onto his back, the very action betraying his need to feel her touch on him. He lay there, still shivering, his eyes closed, his body yielding to her soft, curious hands.

She laid her cheek against his hot skin, awash in new sensations, touches that had been taboo all her life. She was learning his body as a lover would.

"Tell me what to do," she whispered as she drew her cheek against his breastbone. "I'll do anything for you. Anything!"

His hand held hers to him for one long, aching minute. Then he drew it up to his chest and held it there while he struggled to breathe.

Her breasts felt cool as they pressed nakedly into his rib cage where his shirt was pulled away. Her eyes closed and she lay there, close to him, closer to him than she'd ever been.

"Heavens, that was exciting," she choked. "I never dreamed I could touch you like that, and in broad daylight, too!"

That raw innocence caught him off guard. Laughter bubbled up into his chest, into his throat. He began to laugh softly.

"Do hush!" she chided. "What if Mary should hear you and walk in?"

He lifted himself on an elbow and looked down at her bare breasts. "She'd get an eyeful, wouldn't she?" He traced a taut nipple, arrogantly pleased that she didn't object at all.

"I'm small," she whispered.

He smiled. "No, you're not."

She looked down to where his fingers rested against her pale skin. "Your skin is so dark compared to mine..."

"Especially here, where you're so pale," he breathed. His lips bent to the soft skin he was touching, and he took her inside his mouth, gently suckling her.

She arched up, moaning harshly, her fists clenched beside her head as she tried to deal with the mounting delight of sensation.

He heard that harsh sound and reacted to it immediately. His mouth grew insistent, hot and hungry as it suckled hard at her breast. Her body clenched and suddenly went into a shocking spasm that she couldn't control at all. It never seemed to end, the hot, shameful pleasure he gave her with that intimate caress.

She clutched him, breathless, burying her hot face in his neck while she fought to still her shaking limbs, the faint little gasps that he must certainly be able to hear.

His mouth was tender now, calming rather than stirring. He pressed tender, brief kisses all over her skin, ending only reluctantly at her trembling lips.

Her shamed eyes lifted to his, full of tears that reflected her overwhelmed emotions.

He shook his head, dabbing at them with a handkerchief he drew from his slacks pocket. "Don't cry," he whispered gently. "Your breasts are very, very sensitive. I love the way you react to my mouth on them." He smiled. "It's nothing to worry about."

"It's...natural?" she asked.

His hand smoothed her dark hair. "For a few women, I suppose," he said. He searched her curious eyes. "I've never experienced it like this. I'm glad. There should be at least one or two firsts for me, as well as for you."

"I wish I knew more," she said worriedly.

"You'll learn." His fingers traced her nose, her softly swollen lips. "I missed you."

Her heart felt as if it could fly. She smiled. "Did you, really?"

He nodded. "Not that I wanted to," he added with such disgust that she giggled.

He propped himself on an elbow and stared down at her for a long time, his brows drawn together in deep thought.

She could feel the indecision in him, along with a tension that was new to her. Her soft eyes swept over his dark, lean face and back up to meet his curious gaze.

"You're binding me with velvet ropes," he murmured quietly. "I've never felt like this. I don't know how to handle it."

"Neither do I," she said honestly. She drew a slow breath, aware suddenly of her shameless nudity and the coolness of the air on her skin.

He saw that discomfort and deftly helped her back into her clothes with an economy of movement that was somehow disturbing.

"You make me feel painfully young," she confessed.

"You are," he said without hesitation. His pale eyes narrowed. "This is getting dangerous. I can't keep my hands off you lately. And the last thing on earth I'll ever do is seduce my business partner's only daughter."

"I know that, King," she said with an odd sort of dignity. He got to his feet and she laid down again, watching him rearrange his own shirt and vest and jacket and tie. It was strangely intimate.

He knew that. His eyes smiled, even if his lips didn't.

"What are we going to do?" she added.

He stared down at her with an unnerving intensity. "I wish to God I knew."

He pulled her up beside him. His big hands rested warmly on her shoulders. "Wouldn't you like to go to Europe?" he asked.

Her eyebrows lifted. "What for?"

"You could go to college. Or have a holiday. Lettie could go with you," he suggested, naming her godmother. ''She'd spoil you rotten and you'd come back with a hefty knowledge of history.''

"I don't want to go to Europe, and I'm not all that enthralled with history.''

He sighed. ''Tiffany, I'm not going to sleep with you.''

Her full, swollen lips pouted up at him. ''I haven't asked you to.'' She lowered her eyes. ''But I'm not going to sleep with anyone else. I haven't even thought about anyone else since I was fourteen.''

He felt his mind whirling at the confession. He scowled deeply. He was getting in over his head and he didn't know how to stop. She was too young; years too young. She didn't have the maturity, the poise, the sophistication to survive in his world. He could have told her that, but she wouldn't have listened. She was living in dreams. He couldn't afford to.

He didn't answer her. His hands were deep in his pockets and he was watching her worriedly, amazed at his own headlong fall into ruin. No woman in his experience had ever wound him up to such a fever pitch of desire by just parading around in a silk dress. He'd accused her of tempting him, but it wasn't the whole truth. Ever since the night of her birthday party, he hadn't been able to get her soft body out of his mind. He wanted her violently. He just didn't know what to do about it. Marriage was out of the question, even more so was an affair. Whatever else she was, she was still his business partner's daughter.

"You're brooding," she murmured.

He shrugged. "I can't think of anything better to do," he said honestly. "I'm going away for a while," he added abruptly. "Perhaps this will pass if we ignore it."

So he was still going to fight. She hadn't expected anything else, but she was vaguely disappointed, just the same.

"I can learn," she said.

His eyebrow went up.

"I know how to be a hostess," she continued, as if he'd challenged her. "I already know most of the people in your circle, and in Dad's. I'm not fifteen."

His eyes narrowed. "Tiffany, you may know how to be a hostess, but you haven't any idea in hell how to be a wife," he said bluntly.

Her heart jumped wildly in her chest. "I could learn how to be one."

His face hardened. "Not with me. I don't want to get married. And before you say it," he added, holding up a hand, "yes, I want you. But desire isn't enough. It isn't even a beginning. I may be the first man you've ever wanted, Tiffany, but you aren't the first woman I've wanted."

Chapter Four

The mocking smile on his face made Tiffany livid with jealous rage. She scrambled to her feet, her face red and taut.

"That wasn't necessary!" she flung at him.

"Yes, it was," he replied calmly. "You want to play house. I don't."

Totally at a loss, she knotted her hands at her sides and just stared at him. This sort of thing was totally out of her experience. Her body was all that interested him, and it wasn't enough. She had nothing else to bargain with. She'd lost.

It was a new feeling. She'd always had everything she wanted. Her father had spoiled her rotten. King had been another impossible item on her list of luxuries, but he was telling her that she couldn't have him. Her father couldn't buy him for her. And she couldn't flirt and tease and get him for herself. Defeat was strangely cold. It sat in the pit of her stomach like a black emptiness. She didn't know how to handle it.

And he knew. It was in his pale, glittering eyes, in that faint, arrogant smile on his hard mouth.

She wanted to rant and rave, but it wasn't the sort of behavior that would save the day. She relaxed her hands, and her body, and simply looked at him, full of inadequacies and insecurities that she'd never felt before.

"Perhaps when I'm Carla's age, I'll try again," she said with torn pride and the vestiges of a smile.

He nodded with admiration. "That's the spirit," he said gently.

She didn't want gentleness, or pity. She stuck her hands into her jeans pockets. "You don't have to leave town to avoid me," she said. "Lettie's taking me to New York next week," she lied, having arranged the trip mentally in the past few minutes. Lettie would do anything her godchild asked, and she had the means to travel wherever she liked. Besides, she loved New York.

King's eyes narrowed suspiciously. "Does Lettie know she's going traveling?"

"Of course," she said, playing her part to the hilt.

"Of course." He drew in a heavy breath and slowly let it out. His body was still giving him hell, but he wasn't going to let her know it. Ultimately she was better off out of his life.

"See you," she said lightly.

He nodded. "See you."

And he left.

Late that autumn, Tiffany was walking down a
runway in New York wearing the latest creation of
one David Marron, a young designer whose Span-
ish-inspired fashions were a sensation among buy-
ers. The two had met through a mutual friend of
Lettie's and David had seen incredible possibilities
in Tiffany's long black hair and elegance. He
dressed her in a gown that was reminiscent of lacy
Spanish noblewomen of days long past, and she
brought the house down at his first showing of his
new spring line. She made the cover of a major fashion magazine and jumped from an unknown to a
familiar face in less than six months.

Lettie, with her delicately tinted red hair and twinkling brown eyes, was elated at her accomplishment.
It had hurt her deeply to see Tiffany in such an
agony of pain when she'd approached her godmother and all but begged to be taken out of Texas.
Lettie doted on the younger woman and whisked her
away with a minimum of fuss.

They shared a luxurious Park Avenue apartment
and were seen in all the most fashionable places. In
those few months, Tiffany had grown more sophisticated, more mature—and incredibly more withdrawn. She was ice-cold with men, despite the en-
hancement of her beauty and her elegant figure.
Learning to forget King was a full-time job. She was
still working on it.

Just when she was aching to go home to her father

where her chances of seeing King every week were excellent, a lingerie company offered her a lucrative contract and a two-week holiday filming commercials in Jamaica.

"I couldn't turn it down," she told Lettie with a groan. "What's Dad going to say? I was going to help him with his Christmas party. I won't get home until Christmas Eve. After we get back from Jamaica, I have to do a photo layout for a magazine ad campaign due to hit the stands next spring."

"You did the right thing," Lettie assured her. "My dear, at your age, you should be having fun, meeting people, learning to stand alone." She sighed gently. "Marriage and children are for later, when you're established in a career."

Tiffany turned and stared at the older woman. "You never married."

Lettie smiled sadly. "No. I lost my fiancé in Vietnam. I wasn't able to want anyone else in that way."

"Lettie, that's so sad!"

"One learns to live with the unbearable, eventually. I had my charities to keep me busy. And, of course, I had you," she added, giving her goddaughter a quick hug. "I haven't had a bad life."

"Someday you have to tell me about him."

"Someday, I will. But for now, you go ahead to Jamaica and have a wonderful time filming your commercial."

"You'll come with me?" she asked quickly, faintly worried at the thought of being so far away without any familiar faces.

Lettie patted her hand. "Of course I will. I love Jamaica!"

"I have to call Dad and tell him."

"That might be a good idea. He was complaining earlier in the week that your letters were very far apart."

"I'll do it right now."

She picked up the receiver and dialed her father's office number, twisting the cord nervously while she waited to be put through.

"Hi, Dad!" she said.

"Don't tell me," he muttered. "You've met some dethroned prince and you're getting married in the morning."

She chuckled. "No. I've just signed a contract to do lingerie commercials and we're flying to Jamaica to start shooting."

There was a strange hesitation. "When?"

"Tomorrow morning."

"Well, when will you be back?" he asked.

"In two weeks. But I've got modeling assignments in New York until Christmas Eve," she said in a subdued tone.

"What about my Christmas party?" He sounded resigned and depressed. "I was counting on you to arrange it for me."

"You can have a New Year's Eve party for your clients," she improvised with laughter in her voice. "I'll have plenty of time to put that together before I have to start my next assignment. In fact," she added, "I'm not sure when it will be. The lingerie contract was only for the spring line. They're doing different models for different seasons. I was Spring.''

"I can see why," he murmured dryly. "My daughter, the model." He sighed again. "I should never have let you get on the plane with Lettie. It's her fault. I know she's at the back of it."

"Now, Dad…"

"I'm having her stuffed and hung on my wall when she comes back. You tell her that!"

"You know you're fond of Lettie," she chided, with a wink at her blatantly eavesdropping god-mother.

"I'll have her shot!"

She grimaced and Lettie, reading her expression, chuckled, unabashed by Harrison Blair's fury.

"She's laughing," she told him.

"Tell her to laugh while she can." He hesitated and spoke to someone nearby. "King said to tell you he misses you."

Her heart jumped, but she wasn't leaving herself open to any further humiliation at his hands. "Tell him to pull the other one," she chuckled. "Listen, Dad, I have to go. I'll phone you when we're back from Jamaica."

"Wait a minute. Where in Jamaica, and is Lettie going along?"

"Of course she is! We'll have a ball. Take care, Dad. Bye!"

He was still trying to find out where she was going when she hung up on him. He glanced at King with a grimace.

The younger man had an odd expression on his face. It was one Harrison couldn't remember ever seeing there before.

"She's signed a contract," Harrison said, shoving his hands into his pockets as he glared at the telephone, as if the whole thing had been its fault.

"For what?" King asked.

"Lingerie commercials," his partner said heavily. "Just think, my sheltered daughter will be parading around in sheer nighties for the whole damned world to see!"

"Like hell she will. Where is she?" King demanded.

"On her way to Jamaica first thing in the morning. King," he added when the other man started to leave. "She's of age," he said gently. "She's a woman. I don't have the right to tell her how to live her own life. And neither do you."

"I don't want other men ogling her!"

Harrison just nodded. "I know. I don't, either. But it's her decision."

"I won't let her do it," King said doggedly.

"How do you propose to stop her? You can't do it legally. I don't think you can do it any other way, either."

"Did you tell her what I said?"

Harrison nodded again. "She said to pull the other one."

Pale blue eyes widened with sheer shock. It had

never occured to him that he could lose Tiffany, that she wouldn't always be in Harrison's house waiting for him to be ready to settle down. Now she'd flown the coop and the shoe was on the other foot. She'd discovered the pleasure of personal freedom and she didn't want to settle down.

He glanced at Harrison. "Is she serious about this job? Or is it just another ploy to get my attention?"

The other man chuckled. "I have no idea. But you have to admit, she's a pretty thing. It isn't surprising that she's attracted a modeling agency."

King stared out the window with narrowed, thoughtful eyes. "Then she's thinking about making a career of it."

Harrison didn't tell him that her modeling contract might not last very long. He averted his eyes. "She might as well have a career. If nothing else, it will help her mature."

The other man didn't look at him. "She hasn't grown up yet."

"I know that. It isn't her fault. I've sheltered her from life—perhaps too much. But now she wants to try her wings. This is the best time, before she has a reason to fold them away. She's young and she thinks she has the world at her feet. Let her enjoy it while she can."

King stared down at the carpet. "I suppose that's the wise choice."

"It's the only choice," came the reply. "She'll come home when she's ready."

King didn't say another word about it. He

changed the subject to business and pursued it solemnly.

Meanwhile, Tiffany went to Jamaica and had a grand time. Modeling, she discovered, was hard work. It wasn't just a matter of standing in front of a camera and smiling. It involved wardrobe changes, pauses for the proper lighting and equipment setup, minor irritations like an unexpected burst of wind, and artistic temperament on the part of the cameraman.

Lettie watched from a distance, enjoying Tiffany's enthusiasm for the shoot. The two weeks passed all too quickly, with very little time for sightseeing.

"Just my luck," Tiffany groaned when they were back in New York, "I saw the beach and the hotel and the airport. I didn't realize that every free minute was going to be spent working or resting up for the next day's shoot!"

"Welcome to the world of modeling." Lettie chuckled. "Here, darling, have another celery stick."

Tiffany grimaced, but she ate the veggie platter she was offered without protest.

At night, she lay awake and thought about King. She hadn't believed his teasing assertion that he'd missed her. King didn't miss people. He was entirely self-sufficient. But how wonderful if it had been true.

That daydream only lasted until she saw a tabloid

at the drugstore where she was buying hair care products. There was a glorious color photo of King and Carla right on the front page of one, with the legend, "Do wedding bells figure in future for tycoon and secretary?"

She didn't even pick it up, to her credit. She passed over it as if she hadn't seen it. But she went to bed that evening, she cried all night, almost ruining her face for the next day's modeling session.

Unrequited love took its toll on her in the weeks that followed. The one good thing about misery was that it attracted other miserable people. She annexed one Mark Allenby, a male model who'd just broken up with his long-time girlfriend and wanted a shoulder to cry on. He was incredibly handsome and sensitive, and just what Tiffany needed for her shattered ego.

The fact that he was a wild man was certainly a bonus.

He was the sort of person who'd phone her on the spur of the moment and suggest an evening at a retro beatnik coffeehouse where the patrons read bad poetry. He loved practical jokes, like putting whoopee cushions under a couple posing for a romantic ad.

"I can see why you're single," Tiffany suggested breathlessly when she'd helped him outrun the furious photographer. "And I'll bet you never get to work for *him* again," she indicated the heavyset madman chasing them.

"Yes, I will." He chuckled. "When you make it to my income bracket, you don't have to call photographers to get work. They call you." Mark turned and blew the man a kiss, grabbed Tiffany's hand, and pulled her along to the subway entrance nearby.

"You need a makeover," he remarked on their way back to her apartment.

She stopped and looked up at him. "Why?"

"You look too girlish," he said simply, and smiled. "You need a more haute couture image if you want to grow into modeling."

She grimaced. "I'm not sure I really do, though. I like it all right. But I don't need the money."

"Darling, of course you need the money!"

"Not really. Money isn't worth much when you can't buy what you want with it," she said pointedly.

He pushed back his curly black hair and gave her his famous inscrutable he-man stare. "What do you want that you can't buy?"

"King."

"Of which country?"

She grinned. "Not royalty. That's his name. Kingman. Kingman Marshall."

"The tycoon of the tabloids?" he asked, pursing his chiseled lips. "Well, well, you do aim high, don't you? Mr. Marshall has all the women he wants, thank you. And if you have anything more serious in mind, forget it. His father taught him that marriage is only for fools. Rumor has it that his mother took his old man for every cent he had when she divorced him, and that it drove his father to suicide.''

"Yes, I know," she said dully.

"Not that Marshall didn't get even. You probably heard about that, too."

"Often," she replied. "He actually took his mother to court and charged her with culpability in his father's suicide in a civil case. He won." She shivered, remembering how King had looked after the verdict—and, more importantly, how his mother had looked. She lost two-thirds of her assets and the handsome gigolo that she'd been living with. It was no wonder that King had such a low opinion of marriage, and women.

"Whatever became of the ex-Mrs. Marshall?" he asked aloud.

"She overdosed on drugs and died four years ago," she said.

"A sad end."

"Indeed it was."

"You can't blame Marshall for treating women like individually wrapped candies," he expounded. "I don't imagine he trusts anything in skirts."

"You were talking about a makeover?" she interrupted, anxious to get him off the subject of King before she started screaming.

"I was. I'll take you to my hairdresser. He'll make a new woman of you. Then we'll go shopping for a proper wardrobe."

Her pale eyes glittered with excitement. "This sounds like fun."

"Believe me, it will be," he said with a wicked grin. "Come along, darling."

They spent the rest of the day remaking Tiffany. When he took her out that night to one of the more fashionable nightspots, one of the models she'd worked with didn't even recognize her. It was a compliment of the highest order.

Lettie was stunned speechless.

"It's me," Tiffany murmured impishly, whirling in her black cocktail dress with diamond earrings dripping from her lobes. Her hair was cut very short and feathered toward her gamine face. She had just a hint of makeup, just enough to enhance her high cheekbones and perfect bone structure. She looked expensive, elegant, and six years older than she was.

"I'm absolutely shocked," Lettie said after a minute. "My dear, you are the image of your mother."

Tiffany's face softened. "Am I, really?"

Lettie nodded. "She was so beautiful. I always envied her."

"I wish I'd known her," she replied. "All I have are photographs and vague memories of her singing to me at night."

"You were very young when she died. Harrison never stopped mourning her." Her eyes were sad. "I don't think he ever will."

"You never know about Dad," Tiffany remarked, because she knew how Lettie felt about Harrison.

Not that she was gauche enough to mention, it. "Why don't you go out with us tonight?"

"Three's a crowd, dear. Mark will want you to himself."

"It isn't like that at all," Tiffany said gently. "He's mourning his girlfriend and I'm mourning King. We have broken hearts and our work in common, but not much else. He's a friend—and I mean that quite sincerely."

Lettie smiled. "I'm rather glad. He's very nice. But he'll end up in Europe one day in a villa, and that wouldn't suit you at all."

"Are you sure?"

Lettie nodded. "And so are you, in your heart."

Tiffany glanced at herself in the mirror with a quiet sigh. "Fine feathers make fine birds, but King isn't the sort to be impressed by sophistication or beauty. Besides, the tabloids are already predicting that he's going to marry Carla."

"I noticed. Surely you don't believe it?"

"I don't believe he'll ever marry anyone unless he's trapped into it," Tiffany said honestly, and her eyes were suddenly very old. "He's seen nothing of marriage but the worst side."

"It's a pity about that. It's warped his outlook."

"Nothing will ever change it." She smiled at Lettie. "Sure you won't come with us? You won't be a crowd."

"I won't come tonight. But ask me again."

"You can count on it."

*   *   *

Mark was broody as he picked at his mint ice cream.

"You're worried," Tiffany murmured.

He glanced at her wryly. "No. I'm distraught. My girl is being seen around town with a minor movie star. She seems smitten."

"She may be doing the same thing you're doing," she chided. "Seeing someone just to numb the ache."

He chuckled. "Is that what I'm doing?"

"It's what we're both doing."

He reached his hand across the table and held hers. "I'm sorry we didn't meet three years ago, while I was still heart-whole. You're unique. I enjoy having you around."

"Same here. But friendship is all it can ever be."

"Believe it or not, I know that." He put down his spoon. "What are you doing for Christmas?"

"I'll be trying to get back from a location shoot and praying that none of the airline pilots go on strike," she murmured facetiously.

"New Year's?"

"I have to go home and arrange a business party for my father." She glanced at him and her eyes began to sparkle. "I've had an idea. How would you like to visit Texas?"

His eyebrows arched. "Do I have to ride a horse?"

"Not everyone in Texas rides. We live in Jacobsville. It's not too far from San Antonio. Dad's in business there."

"Jacobsville." He fingered his wineglass with elegant dark fingers that looked very sexy in the ads he modeled for. "Why not? It's a long way from Manhattan."

"Yes, it is, and I can't bear to go home alone."

"May I ask why?"

"Of course. My own heartbreaker lives there. I told you about him. I ran away from home so that I could stop eating my heart out over him. But memories and heartache seem to be portable," she added heavily.

"I could attest to that myself." He looked up at her with wickedly twinkling black eyes. "And what am I going to be? The competition?"

"Would you mind?" she asked. "I'll gladly do the same for you anytime you like. I need your moral support."

He paused thoughtfully and then he smiled. "You know, this might be the perfect answer to both our headaches. All right. I'll do it." He finished his wine.

"I've been asked to fill a lot of roles. That's a new one." He lifted his glass and took a sip. "What the hell. I'll tangle with Kingman Marshall. I don't want to live forever. I'm yours, darling. At least, for the duration of the party," he added with a grin.

She lifted her own glass. "Here's to pride."

He answered the toast. As she drank it, she wondered how she was going to bear seeing King with Carla. At least she'd have company and camouflage. King would never know that her heart was breaking.

Chapter Five

Tiffany and Mark boarded the plane with Lettie the day before New Year's Eve. Tiffany looked sleek and expensive in a black figure-hugging suit with silver accessories and a black-and-white striped scarf draped over one shoulder. Mark, in a dark suit, was the picture of male elegance. Women literally sighed when he walked past. It was odd to see a man that handsome in person, and Tiffany enjoyed watching people react to him.

Lettie sat behind them and read magazines while Mark and Tiffany discussed their respective assignments and where they might go next.

It wasn't as long a flight as she'd expected it to be. They walked onto the concourse at the San Antonio airport just in time for lunch.

Tiffany had expected her father to meet them, and sure enough, he was waiting near the gate. Tiffany ran to him to be hugged and kissed warmly before she introduced Mark.

Harrison scowled as he shook hands with the young man, but he gathered his composure quickly and the worried look vanished from his features. He greeted Lettie warmly, too, and led the three of them to the limousine near the front entrance.

"Mark's staying with us, Dad," Tiffany said. "We're both working for the same agency in Manhattan and our holidays coincided."

"We'll be glad to have you, Mark," Harrison said with a forced warmth that only Tiffany seemed to notice.

"How is King?" Lettie asked.

Harrison hesitated with a lightning glance at Tiffany. "He's fine. Shall we go?"

Tiffany wondered why her father was acting so peculiarly, but she pretended not to be interested in King or his feelings. Only with Mark.

"Did you manage to get the arrangements finalized?" Harrison asked his daughter.

She grinned. "Of course. Long distance isn't so long anymore, and it wasn't that hard. I've dealt with the same people for years arranging these 'do's' for you. The caterer, the flowers, the band, even the invitations are all set."

"You're sure?" Harrison murmured.

She nodded. "I'm sure."

"You didn't forget to send an invitation to King and Carla?" her father added.

"Of course not! Theirs were the first to go out,"

she said with magnificent carelessness. "I wouldn't forget your business partner."

Harrison seemed to relax just a little.

"What's wrong?" she asked, sensing some problem.

"He's out of town," he said reluctantly. "Rather, they're out of town, and not expected back until sometime next week. Or so King's office manager said. I hadn't heard from him, and I wondered why he was willing to forgo the party. He never misses the holiday bash. Or, at least, he never has before."

Tiffany didn't betray her feelings by so much as the batting of an eyelash how much that statement hurt. She only smiled. "I suppose he had other plans and wasn't willing to change them."

"Perhaps so," he said, but he didn't look convinced.

Mark reached beside him and caught Tiffany's hand in his, pressing it reassuringly. He seemed to sense, as her father did, how miserable she felt at King's defection. But Mark asked Harrison a question about a landmark he noticed as they drove down the long highway that would carry them to Jacobsville, and got him off on a subject dear to his heart. By the time they reached the towering brick family home less than an hour later, Mark knew more about the siege at the Alamo than he'd ever gleaned from books.

Tiffany was too busy with her arrangements to keep Mark company that day or the next, so he borrowed a sedan from the garage and set about learning the area. He came back full of tidbits about the history of the countryside, which he seemed to actually find fascinating.

He watched Tiffany directing the traffic of imported people helping with the party with amused indulgence.

"You're actually pretty good at this," he murmured. "Where did you learn how to do it?"

She looked surprised. "I didn't. It just seemed to come naturally. I love parties."

"I don't," he mused. "I usually become a decoration."

She knew what he meant. She learned quickly that very few of the parties models attended were anything but an opportunity for designers to show off their fashions in a relaxed setting. The more wealthy clients who were present, the better the opportunity to sell clothes. But some of the clients found the models more interesting than their regalia. Tiffany had gravitated toward Mark for mutual protection at first. Afterward, they'd become fast friends.

"You won't be a decoration here," she promised him with a smile. "What do you think?"

She swept her hand toward the ballroom, which was polished and packed with flowers and long tables with embroidered linen tablecloths, crystal and china and candelabras. Buffets would be set up there for snacks, because it wasn't a sit-down dinner. There would be dancing on the highly polished floor to music provided by a live band, and mixed drinks would be served at the bar.

"It's all very elegant," Mark pronounced.

She nodded absently, remembering other parties when she'd danced and danced, when King had been close at hand to smile at her and take her out onto the dance floor. She hadn't danced with him often, but each time was indelibly imprinted in her mind. She could close her eyes and see him, touch him. She sighed miserably. Well, she might as well stop looking back. She had to go on, and King wanted no part of her. His absence from this most special of all parties said so.

"I think it'll do," she replied after a minute. She gave him a warm smile. "Come on and I'll show you the way I've decorated the rest of the house."

Tiffany wore a long silver-sequined dress for the party, with a diamond clip in her short hair. She'd learned how to walk, how to move, how to pose, and even people who'd known her for years were taken aback at her new image.

Mark, at her side, resplendent in dark evening dress, drew feminine eyes with equal magnetism. His Italian ancestry was very evident in his liquid black eyes and olive complexion and black, black hair. One of Tiffany's acquaintances, a pretty little redhead named Lisa, seemed to be totally captivated by Mark. She stood in a corner by herself, just staring at him.

"Should I take pity on her and introduce you?" she asked Mark in a teasing whisper.

He glanced toward the girl, barely out of her

teens, and she blushed as red as her hair. Seconds later, she rushed back toward her parents. He chuckled softly.

"She's very young," he mused. "A friend?"

She shook her head. "Her parents are friends of my father's. Lisa is a loner. As a rule, she doesn't care as much for dating as she does for horses. Her family has stables and they breed racehorses."

"Well, well. All that, and no beaux?"

"She's shy with men."

His eyebrows arched. He looked at the young woman a second time, and his eyes narrowed as they caught her vivid blue ones and held them relentlessly. Lisa spilled her drink and blushed again, while her mother fussed at the skirt of her dress with a handkerchief.

"How wicked," Tiffany chided to Mark.

"Eyes like hers should be illegal," he murmured, but he was still staring at Lisa just the same. He took Tiffany's arm and urged her toward the group. "Introduce me."

"Don't..." she began.

"I'm not that much a rake." He calmed her. "She intrigues me. I won't take advantage. I promise." He smiled, although his eyes were solemn.

"All right, then." She stopped at Mrs. McKinley's side. "Will it stain?" she asked gently.

"Oh, I don't think so," the older woman said with a smile. "It was mostly ice. Lisa, you remember our Tiffany, don't you?" she added.

Lisa looked up, very flustered as her eyes darted

nervously from Mark's to Tiffany. "H...hi, Tiffany. Nice to see you."

"Nice to see you, Lisa," Tiffany replied with a genuine smile. "I'm sorry about your dress. Have you met Mark Allenby? He works with me. We're both represented by the same modeling agency in New York. You might have seen him in the snack food commercials with the puppet...?"

"G...good Lord, was that you?" Lisa choked. "I thought he...you...looked familiar, Mr. Allenby!"

He smiled lazily. "Nice of you to remember it, Miss McKinley. Do you dance?"

She looked as if she might faint. "Well, yes..."

He held out a hand. "You'll excuse me?" he said to Tiffany and Lisa's parents.

Lisa put her hand into his and let him lead her onto the dance floor. Her eyes were so full of dreams and delight that Mark couldn't seem to stop looking down at her.

"He dances beautifully," Mrs. McKinley said.

"Not bad," her gruff husband agreed. "Is he gay?"

"Mark?" Tiffany chuckled. "Not a chance. He's quite a success story, in fact. His parents are Italian. He came to this country as a baby and his father held down two jobs while his mother worked as a waitress in a cafeteria. He makes enough to support both of them now, and his three young sisters. He's very responsible, loyal, and not a seducer of innocents, just in case you wondered."

Mrs. McKinley colored. "I'm sorry, but he was

an unknown quantity, and it's very easy to see the effect he has on Lisa.''

"I wouldn't worry," she said gently. "He's just broken up with his long-time girlfriend and his heart hurts. He's not in the market for an affair, anyway.''

"That's a relief,'' the older woman said with a smile. "She's so unworldly.''

Because she'd been as sheltered as Tiffany herself had. There were great disadvantages to that over-protection in today's world, Tiffany thought miserably. She stared into her champagne and wondered why King had declined the invitation to the party. Perhaps he was making the point that he could do nicely without Tiffany. If so, he'd succeeded beyond his wildest dreams.

She got through the long evening on champagne and sheer willpower. Mark seemed to be enjoying himself immensely. He hardly left Lisa all evening, and when she and her parents got ready to leave, he held onto her hand as if he couldn't bear to let it go.

They spoke in terse, quiet tones and as she left, her blue eyes brightened considerably, although Mrs. McKinley looked worried.

"I'm going over there tomorrow to see their horses. You don't mind?" he asked Tiffany as the other guests were preparing to leave.

She stared up at him curiously. "She's very young.''

"And innocent,'' he added, his hands deep in his pockets. "You don't need to tell me that. I haven't ever known anyone like her. She's the sort of girl I might have met back home, if my parents hadn't immigrated to America.''

She was startled. ''I thought you were grinding your teeth over your girlfriend?''

He smiled vaguely. ''So did I.'' His head turned toward the front door. ''She's breakable,'' he said softly. ''Vulnerable and sweet and shy.'' His broad shoulders rose and fell. ''Strange. I never liked red-heads before.''

Tiffany bit her lower lip. She didn't know how to put into words what she was feeling. Lisa was the sort of girl who'd never get over having her hopes raised and then dashed. Did he know that?

''She dances like a fairy,'' he murmured, turning away, his dark eyes introspective and oblivious to the people milling around him.

Harrison joined his daughter at the door as the last guests departed.

''Your friend seems distracted,'' he murmured, his eyes on Mark, who was staring out a darkened window.

''Lisa affected him.''

''I noticed. So did everybody else. He's a rake.''

She shook her head. ''He's a hardworking man with deep family ties and an overworked sense of responsibility. He's no rake.''

''I thought you said he had a girlfriend.''

''She dumped him for somebody richer,'' she said simply. ''His pride was shattered. That's why he's here with me. He couldn't bear seeing her around town in all the nightspots with her new lover.''

Harrison's attitude changed. ''Poor guy.''

''He won't hurt Lisa,'' she assured him, mentally crossing her fingers. She saw trouble ahead, but she didn't know quite how to ward it off.

He studied her face. ''You're much more mature. I wouldn't have recognized you.'' He averted his eyes. ''Pity King didn't get back in time for the party.''

She froze over. ''I didn't expect him, so it's no great loss.''

He started to speak, and suddenly closed his mouth. He smiled at her. ''Let's have a nightcap. Your friend can come along.''

She took his arm with a grin. ''That sounds more like you!''

The next day, Mark borrowed Harrison's sedan again and made a beeline for the McKinley place outside town. He was wearing slacks and a turtle-neck white sweater and he looked both elegant and expensive.

As Tiffany stood on the porch waving him off, a car came purring up the driveway. It was a black Lincoln. She fought down the urge to run. She didn't have to back away from King anymore. She was out of his reach. She folded her arms over the red silk blouse she was wearing with elegant black slacks and leaned against a post in a distinctive pose to wait for him. It surprised her just a little that he didn't have Carla with him.

King took the steps two at a time. He was wearing dark evening clothes, as if he'd just come from a party. She imagined he was still wearing the clothes he'd had on the night before. Probably he didn't keep anything to change into at Carla's place, she thought venomously, certain that it explained his state of dress.

"Well, well, what brings you here?" she drawled, without any particular shyness.

King paused at the last step, scowling as he got a good look at her. The change was phenomenal. She wasn't the young girl he'd left behind months before. She was poised, elegant, somehow cynical. Her eyes were older and there was no welcome or hero-worship in them now. Her smile, if anything, was mocking.

"I came to see Harrison," he said curtly.

She waved a hand toward the front door. "Help yourself. I was just seeing Mark off."

He seemed suddenly very still. "Mark?"

"Mark Allenby. We work together. He came home with me for our holidays." She gave him a cool glance. "You've probably seen him in commercials. He's incredibly handsome."

He didn't say another word. He walked past her without speaking and went right into the house.

Tiffany followed a few minutes later, and found him with her father in the study.

Harrison glanced out the door as she passed it on

her way to the staircase. "Tiffany! Come in here a minute, would you, sweetheart?"

He never called her pet names unless he wanted something. She wandered into the room as if King's presence made no difference at all to her. "What do you want, Dad?" she asked with a smile.

"King needs some papers from the safe at my office, and I promised I'd drive Lettie down to Floresville to visit her sister. Would you...?"

She knew the combination by heart, something her father had entrusted her with only two years before. But she sensed a plot here and she hesitated. King noticed, and his face froze over.

"You don't have anything pressing, do you?" Harrison persisted. "Not with Mark away?"

"I suppose not." She gave in. "I'll just get my jacket."

"Thanks, sweetheart!"

She only shrugged. She didn't even glance at King.

It was a short drive to the downtown office her father shared with King. It seemed a little strange to her that King didn't have the combination to Harrison's safe, since they were partners. She'd never really wondered why until now.

"Doesn't he trust you?" she chided as they went into the dark office together.

"As much as he trusts anyone," he replied. "But in case you wondered, he doesn't have the combination to my safe, either. Our respective lawyers have both. It's a safeguard, of a sort.''

He turned on the lights and closed the door. The sprawling offices were vacant on this holiday and she was more aware than ever of being totally alone with him. It shouldn't have bothered her, knowing what she did about his relationship with Carla, but it did. It hadn't been long enough for her to forget the pleasure of his kisses, being in his arms.

She ignored her tingling nerves and went straight to the concealed safe, opening it deftly. "What do you want out of here?" she asked.

"A brown envelope marked Internet Proposals."

She searched through the documents and found what he wanted. She closed the safe, replaced the painting that covered it, and handed the envelope to King.

"Is that all you needed me for?" she asked, turning toward the door.

"Not quite."

She hesitated a few feet away from him. Her eyes asked the question for her.

He wasn't smiling. The friendly man of years past was missing. His eyes were wary and piercing. He didn't move at all. He just stared at her until she felt her heartbeat accelerate.

She lifted her chin. "Well?"

"Was it deliberate?"

She blinked. "Was what deliberate?"

"Leaving us off the guest list for the New Year's Eve party."

She felt an uncomfortable tension in the air. She frowned. "You and Carla were invited," she said. "I faxed the list of invitations straight to the printers. The two of you were the first two names on the list. In fact, they went straight to my father's secretary from the printer's, to be mailed. Carla knows Rita, Dad's secretary. I'm sure she knew that you were on the list."

His eyes narrowed. "She said that she checked the list. Our names weren't there."

"Someone's lying," Tiffany said quietly.

He made a sound deep in his throat. "I don't need two guesses for a name."

"You think I did it. Why?"

He shrugged. "Spite?" he asked with a mocking smile. "After all, I sent you packing, didn't I?"

Months of conditioning kept her face from giving away any of her inner feelings. She pushed a hand into her jacket pocket and lifted an eyebrow. "You did me a favor, as it happens," she said. "You needn't worry, I'm no longer a threat to you. Mark and I are quite an item about town these days. We both work for the same agency. We see a lot of each other. And not only on the job."

His narrow gaze went over her, looking for differences. "You've changed."

Her shoulders rose and fell. "I've only grown up." Her smile never reached her eyes. "I have a bright future, they tell me. It seems that my body is photogenic."

Something flashed in his eyes and he turned away

before she could see it. "I thought you were going on a holiday, not to find a job."

"I didn't have much choice," she said, turning back to the door. "There was nothing for me here."

His fist clenched at his side. He turned, about to speak, but she'd already opened the door and gone out into the hall.

He followed her, surprised to find her headed not for the exit, but for Rita's computer. She sat down behind the desk that her father's secretary used, turned on the computer, fed in a program, and searched the files for the invitation list. She found it and pulled it up on the screen. Sure enough, King's name wasn't on it. Neither was Carla's. But one of the agency models was a computer whiz and she'd been tutoring Tiffany on the side.

"I told you our names weren't there," he said gruffly from behind her.

"Oh, don't give up yet. Wait just a sec..." She put up another program, one designed to retrieve lost files, and set it searching. A minute later, she pulled up the deleted file and threw it up on the screen. There, at the top of the list, were King's and Carla's names.

King scowled. "How did you do that? I didn't see your hands typing on the keyboard."

"They didn't. This file was deliberately erased and replaced. I'm sure if I look for the fax, I'll discover that it's been redone as well." She saved the file, cut off the computer, and got to her feet. She met his eyes coldly. "Tell Carla nice try. But next time, she'd better practice a little more on her technique."

She retrieved her purse and went out the door, leaving King to follow, deep in thought.

"Why do you think Carla tampered with the list?" he asked on the way home.

"She's a girl with aspirations. Not that I'm any threat to them," she added firmly. "I have a life in New York that I'm learning to love, and a man to shower affection on. You might tell her that, before she dreams up any new ideas to put me in a bad light."

He didn't answer her. But his hands tightened on the steering wheel.

She was out of the car before he could unfasten his seatbelt.

The house was empty, she knew, because Harrison was supposed to be out, and she was certain that Mark was still at Lisa's house. She didn't want King inside.

She paused on the lowest step. "I'll tell Dad you got the information you needed," she said firmly.

His narrow eyes went from her to the front of the house. "Is he in there waiting for you?" he asked coldly.

"If he is, it's nothing to do with you," she said solemnly. "As you said on that most memorable occasion, I wanted to play house and you didn't. For the record," she added with cold eyes, "I no longer want to play with you, in any manner whatsoever. Goodbye.''

She went to the door, unlocked it, let herself in, and threw the bolt home after her. If he heard it, so much the better. She didn't want him within three feet of her, ever again!

Chapter Six

Tiffany went upstairs, almost shaking with fury at Carla's treacherous action, because certainly no one else could be blamed for the omission of those names on the guest list. Carla was playing to win and thought Tiffany was competition. It was funny, in a way, because King wanted no part of her. Why didn't Carla know that?

She went into her room and opened her closet. It was New Year's Day, and tomorrow she and Mark would have to fly back to New York and get ready to begin work again. It was going to be a hectic few weeks, with the Spring showings in the near future, and Tiffany was almost certain that she'd be able to land a new contract. She was young and photogenic and her agent said that she had great potential. It wasn't as heady a prospect as a life with King, but it would have to suffice. Loneliness was something she was just going to have to get used to, so she...

"Packing already?"

The drawled question surprised her into gasping. She whirled, a hand at her throat, to find King lounging in the doorway.

"How did you get in?" she demanded.

"Kitty let me in the back door. She's cleaning the kitchen." He closed the door firmly behind him and started toward Tiffany with a strange glitter in his pale blue eyes. "It isn't like you to run from a fight. You never used to."

"Maybe I'm tired of fighting," she said through a tight throat.

"Maybe I am, too," he replied curtly.

He backed her against the bed and suddenly gave her a gentle push. She went down onto the mattress and his lean, hard body followed her. He braced himself on his forearms beside her head and stared into her eyes at a breathless proximity.

"I'm expecting Mark..." She choked.

"Really? Kitty says he's at Lisa McKinley's house, and very smitten, too, from the look of them at the party last night." His hand smoothed away the lapels of her jacket. His big hand skimmed softly over her breast and his thumb lingered there long enough to make the tip go hard. He smiled when he felt it. "Some things, at least, never change."

"I don't know what you...oh!"

She arched completely off the bed when his mouth suddenly covered her breast. Even through two layers of cloth, it made her shiver with pleasure.

Her hands clenched at her ears and her eyes closed as she gave in without even a struggle.

His hands slid under her clothing to the two fastenings at her back. He loosened them and his hands found the softness of her breasts. "Good God, it's like running my hands over silk," he whispered as his head lifted. "You feel like sweet heaven."

As he spoke, his hands moved. He watched her pupils dilate, her lips part on whispery little sighs that grew sharp when his thumbs brushed her hard nipples.

"The hell with it," he murmured roughly. He sat up, drawing her with him, and proceeded to undress her.

"King...you can't...!"

"I want to suckle you," he said quietly, staring into her shocked eyes as he freed her body from the clothes.

The words fanned the flames that were already devouring her. She didn't speak again. She sat breathing like a track runner while he tossed her jacket and blouse and bra off the bed. Then his hands at her rib cage arched her delicately toward him. He bent and his mouth slowly fastened on her breast.

There was no past, no present. There was only the glory of King's hard mouth on her body. She sobbed breathlessly as the pleasure grew to unbelievable heights.

He had her across his knees, her head falling naturally into the crook of his arm, while he fed on her breasts. The nuzzling, suckling pressure was the sweetest sensation she'd ever known. It had been so long since he'd held her like this. She was alive again, breathing again.

"Easy, darling," he whispered when she began to sob aloud. "Easy, now."

"King...!" Her voice broke. She sounded as frantic as she felt, her heartbeat smothering her, the pressure of his hands all of heaven as he held her to his chest.

"Baby..." He eased her onto the bed and slid alongside her, his face solemn, his eyes dark with feeling. His mouth found hers, held it gently under his while his hands searched out the places where she ached and began to soothe them...only the soothing made the tension worse.

She moaned, tears of frustration stinging her eyes as his caresses only made the hunger more unbearable.

"All right," he whispered, easing down against her. "It's too soon, Tiffany, but I'm going to give you what you want."

He shifted her and his hand moved slowly against her body. She stiffened, but he didn't stop. He kissed her shocked eyelids closed and then smothered the words of protest she tried to voice.

She had no control over her body, none at all. It insisted, it demanded, it was wanton as it sought fulfillment. Her eyes remained tightly closed while she arched and arched, pleading, whispering to him, pride shorn from her in the grip of a madness like none she'd ever experienced.

She opened her eyes all at once and went rigid as a flash of pleasure like hot lightning shot through her flesh. She looked at him in shock and awe and suddenly she was flying among the stars, falling, soaring, in a shuddering ecstasy that none of her reading had ever prepared her for.

Afterward, of course, she wept. She was embarrassed and shocked by this newest lesson in passion and its fulfillment. She hid her face against him, still shivering gently in the aftermath.

"I told you it was too soon," he whispered quietly. He held her close, his face nuzzling her throat. "I took it too far. I only meant to kiss you." His arms tightened. "Don't cry. There's no reason to be upset."

"Nobody...*ever*..." She choked.

His thumb pressed against her swollen lips. "I know." His mouth moved onto her wet eyelids and kissed the tears away slowly. "And that was only the beginning," he whispered. "You can't imagine how it really feels."

He carried her hand to his body and shivered as he moved it delicately against him. "I want you."

She pressed her lips to his throat. "I know. I want you, too."

His teeth nipped her earlobe gently and his breath caught. "Tiffany, your father is my business partner. There's no way we can sleep together without having him find out. It would devastate him. He doesn't really belong to this century."

"I know." She grimaced slightly. "Neither do I, I suppose."

He lifted his head and looked down at her soft hand resting so nervously against his body. He smiled gently even through the pleasure of her touch. His hand pressed hers closer as he looked into her eyes hungrily. "I'm starving," he whispered.

She swallowed, gathering her nerve. "I could…?"

He sighed. "No. You couldn't." He took her hand away and held it tightly in his. "In my way, I'm pretty old-fashioned, too." He grimaced. "I suppose you'd better come into town with me tomorrow and pick out a ring."

Her eyelids fluttered. "A what?"

"An engagement ring and a wedding band," he continued.

"You don't want to marry. You said so."

He looked down at himself ruefully and then back at her flushed face. "It's been several months," he said pointedly. "I'm not a man to whom abstinence comes naturally, to put it modestly. I need a woman."

"I thought you were having Carla," she accused.

He sighed heavily. "Well, that's one of the little problems I've been dealing with since you left. She can't seem to arouse my…interest."

Her eyes widened. This was news. "I understood that any woman can arouse a man."

"Reading fiction again, are we?" he murmured dryly. "Well, books and instruction manuals notwithstanding, my body doesn't seem to be able to read. It only wants you. And it wants you violently."

She was still tingling from her own pleasure. She grimaced.

"What?" he asked.

"I feel guilty. This was all just for me," she faltered, still a little embarrassed.

"I'll run around the house three times and have a cold shower," he murmured dryly. "No need to fret."

She laid back on the bed, watching him sketch her nudity with quick, possessive eyes. "You can, if you want to," she whispered with a wicked smile, never so sure of him as she was at the moment. "I'll let you."

His high cheekbones actually flushed. "With Kitty in the kitchen and aware that I'm up here?" He smiled mockingly and glanced at his watch. "I'd say we have about two minutes to go."

"Until what?"

"Until you have a phone call, or I have a phone call," he remarked. "Which will have strangely been disconnected the minute we pick up the receiver."

She giggled. "You're kidding."

"I'm not." He got up and rearranged his tie, staring down at her with pure anguish. "I want to bury myself in you!" he growled softly.

She flushed. "King!"

It didn't help that her eyes went immediately to that part of him that would perform such a task and she went even redder. She threw herself off the bed and began to fumble to put her clothing back on.

He chuckled. "All that magnificent bravado, gone without a whimper. What a surprise you've got in store on our wedding night," he murmured.

She finished buttoning her blouse and gave him a wry look. "You really are a rake."

"And you'll be glad about that, too," he added with a knowing look. "I promise you will."

She moved close to him, her eyes wide and eloquent. "It won't hurt after what we've done, will it?"

He hesitated. "I don't know," he said finally. "I'll be as careful and gentle as I can."

"I know that." She searched his eyes with a deep sadness that she couldn't seem to shake. "It's only because you want me that we're getting married, isn't it?"

He scowled. "Don't knock it. Sex is the foundation of any good marriage. You and I are highly compatible in that respect."

She wanted to pursue the conversation, but there was a sudden knock at the door.

"Yes, what is it, Kitty?" Tiffany called, distracted.

"Uh, there's a phone call for Mr. Marshall, Miss Tiffany," she called nervously.

"I'll take it downstairs, Kitty. Thanks!" he added with a roguish look in Tiffany's direction.

"You're welcome!" Kitty called brightly, and her footsteps died away.

"Your father puts her up to that," he mused.

"He's sheltered me."

"I know."

She pursed her lips and eyed him mischievously. "I've been saved up for you."

"I'll be worth the effort," he promised, a dark, confident gleam in his eyes.

"Oh, I know that." She went to open the door, pushing back her disheveled hair. "Are you coming to dinner tonight?"

"Is your male fashion plate going to be here?"

"I'm not sure. Lisa was very taken with him, and vice versa."

He smiled. "I started up here bristling with jealousy. I could have danced a jig when Kitty stopped me to tell me about your houseguest and Lisa."

"You were jealous?" she asked.

He lifted an eyebrow and his eyes slid over her like hands. "We both know that you've belonged to me since you've had breasts," he said blatantly. "I kept my distance, almost for too long. But I came to my senses in time."

"I hope you won't regret it."

"So do I," he said without thinking, and he looked disturbed.

"I'll try to make you glad," she whispered in what she hoped was a coquettish tone.

He grinned. "See that you do."

She opened the door and he followed her out into the hall.

Mark was more amused than anything when he discovered that his gal pal was engaged to her dream man. He and Lisa had found many things in common and a romance was blooming there, so he had only good wishes for Tiffany and her King. But there was something in the way King looked that made him uneasy. That man didn't have happily ever after in mind, and he wasn't passionately in love with Tiffany—and it showed. He wanted her; that was obvious to a blind man. But it seemed less than honest for a man to marry a woman only because of desire. Perhaps her father was the fly in the ointment. He couldn't see the dignified Mr. Blair allowing his only daughter to become the mistress of his business partner.

Of course! That had to be the reason for the sudden marriage plans. King had manipulated Tiffany so that she was done out of a fairy tale wedding, so that she was settling for a small, intimate ceremony instead. It was unkind and Mark wished he could help, but it seemed the only thing he could do for his friend was wish her the best and step aside. King didn't seem like a man who'd want a male friend in his virgin bride's life....

Life changed for Tiffany overnight. She went to one of the biggest jewelers in San Antonio with

King, where they looked at rings for half an hour before she chose a wide antique gold wedding band in yellow and white gold, with engraved roses.

King hesitated. "Don't you want a diamond?" he asked.

"No." She wasn't sure why, but she didn't. She let the salesman try the ring on her finger. It was a perfect fit and she was enchanted with it.

King held her hand in his and looked down at it. The sentiment of the old-fashioned design made him strangely uneasy. It looked like an heirloom, something a wife would want to pass down to a child. His eyes met hers and he couldn't hide his misgivings. He'd more or less been forced into proposing by the situation, but he hadn't thought past the honeymoon. Here was proof that Tiffany had years, not months, of marriage in mind, while he only wanted to satisfy a raging hunger.

"Don't you like it?" she asked worriedly.

"It's exquisite," he replied with a determined smile. "Yes, I like it."

She sighed, relieved. "Don't you want to choose one?" she asked when he waved the salesman away.

"No," he said at once. He glanced down at her. "I'm not much on rings. I'm allergic to gold," he added untruthfully, thinking fast.

"Oh. Oh, I see." She brightened a little. It had hurt to think he didn't want to wear a visible symbol of his married status.

In no time at all, they were caught up in wedding arrangements. King didn't want a big society wedding, and neither did Tiffany. They settled for a small, intimate service in the local Presbyterian church with friends and family. A minister was engaged, and although traditionally the groom was to provide the flowers, Tiffany made the arrangements for them to be delivered.

Her one regret was not being able to have the elegant wedding gown she'd always imagined that she'd have. Such a dress seemed somehow out of place at a small service. She chose to wear a modern designer suit in white, instead, with an elegant little hat and veil.

She wished that her long-time best friend hadn't married a military man and moved to Germany with him. She had no one to be maid or matron of honor. There again, in a small service it wouldn't be noticeable.

King became irritable and withdrawn as the wedding date approached. He was forever away on business or working late at the office, and Tiffany hoped this wasn't going to become a pattern for their married life. She was realistic enough to understand that his job was important to him, but she wanted a big part in his life. She hoped she was going to have one.

The night before the wedding, King had supper with Tiffany and her father. He was so remote even Harrison noticed.

"Not getting cold feet, are you?" Harrison

teased, and tensed at the look that raced across the younger man's face before he could conceal it.

"Of course not," King said curtly. "I've had a lot on my mind lately, that's all."

Tiffany paused with her glass in midair to glance at King. She hadn't really noticed how taut his face was, how uneasy he seemed. He'd never spoken of marriage in anyone's memory. In fact, he'd been quite honest about his mistrust of it. He'd had girlfriends for as long as Tiffany could remember, but there had never been a reason to be jealous of any of them. King never let himself become serious over a woman.

"Don't drop that," King murmured, nodding toward the loose grip she had on the glass.

She put it down deliberately. "King, you do want to marry me, don't you?" she asked abruptly.

His eyes met hers across the table. There was no trace of expression in them. "I wouldn't have asked you if I hadn't meant to go through with it," he replied.

The phrasing was odd. She hesitated for a few seconds, tracing patterns on her glass. "I could work for a while longer," she suggested, "and we could put off the ceremony."

"We're getting married Saturday," he reminded her. "I already have tickets for a resort on Jamaica for our honeymoon. We're scheduled on a nonstop flight Saturday afternoon to Montego Bay."

"Plans can be changed," she replied.

He laughed humorlessly. "Now who's got cold feet?" he challenged.

"Not me," she lied. She smiled and drained her glass. But inside, butterflies were rioting in her stomach. She'd never been more unsure of her own hopes and dreams. She wanted King, and he wanted her. But his was a physical need. Had she pushed him into this marriage after all, and now he was going to make the most of it? What if he tired of her before the honeymoon was even over?

She stopped this train of thought. It was absurd to have so little faith in her own abilities. She'd vamped him at her twenty-first birthday party, to such effect that he'd come home from his business trip out of his mind over her. If she could make him crazy once, she could do it twice. She could make him happy. She could fit in his world. It was, after all, hers, too. As for Carla, and the complications she might provoke, she could worry about that later. If she could keep King happy at home, Carla wouldn't have a prayer of splitting them up.

Her covetous eyes went over him as if they were curious hands, searching out his chiseled mouth, his straight nose, the shape of his head, the darkness of his hair, the deep-set eyes that could sparkle or stun. He was elegant, devastating to look at, a physical presence wherever he went. He had power and wealth and the arrogance that went with them. But was he capable of love, with the sort of loveless background he'd had? Could he learn it?

As she studied him, his head turned and he studied her, his eyes admiring her beauty, her grace. Something altered in the eyes that swept over her and his eyes narrowed.

"Am I slurping my soup?" she asked with an impish grin.

Caught off guard, he chuckled. "No. I was thinking what a beauty you are," he said honestly. "You won't change much in twenty years. You may get a gray hair or two, but you'll still be a miracle."

"What a nice thing to say," she murmured, putting down her soup spoon. "You remember that, in about six years' time. I'll remind you, in case you forget."

"I won't forget," he mused.

Harrison let out a faint sigh of relief. Surely it was only prenuptial nerves eating at King. The man had known Tiffany for years, after all, there wouldn't be many surprises for them. They had things in common and they liked each other. Even if love was missing at first, he knew it would come. It would have to. Nothing short of it would hold a man like King.

Tiffany glanced at her father's somber expression and lifted an eyebrow. "It's a wedding, not a wake," she chided.

He jerked and then laughed. "Sorry, darling, I was miles away."

"Thinking about Lettie?" she teased.

He glared at her. "I was not," he snapped back. "If they ever barbecue her, I'll bring the sauce."

"You know you like her. You're just too stubborn to admit it."

"She's a constant irritation, like a mole at the belt line."

Tiffany's eyes widened. "What a comparison!"

"I've got a better one," he said darkly.

"Don't say it!"

"Spoilsport," he muttered, attacking his slice of apple pie as if it were armed.

King was listening to the byplay, not with any real interest. He was deeply thoughtful and unusually quiet. He glanced at Tiffany occasionally, but now his expression was one of vague concern and worry. Was he keeping something from her? Perhaps something was going on in his life that she didn't know about. If she could get him alone later, perhaps he'd tell her what it was.

But after they finished eating, King glanced quickly at his watch and said that he had to get back to the office to finish up some paperwork.

Tiffany got up from the table and followed him into the hallway. "I thought we might have a minute to talk," she said worriedly. "We're getting married tomorrow."

"Which is why I have to work late tonight," he replied tersely. "It's been a very long time since I've given myself a week off. Ask your father."

"I don't have to. I know how hard you work." She looked up at him with real concern. "There's still time to back out, if you want to."

His eyebrows shot up. "Do you want to?"

She gnawed the inside of her lip, wondering if that was what he wanted her to admit. It was so difficult trying to read his thoughts. She couldn't begin to.

"No," she said honestly. "I don't want to. But if you do…"

"We'll go through with it," he said. "After all, we've got plenty in common. And it will keep the business in the family."

"Yes, it will go to our children…" she began.

"Good God," he laughed without mirth, "don't start talking about a family! That's years away, for us." He scowled suddenly and stared at her. "You haven't seen a doctor, have you?"

"For the blood test," she reminded him, diverted.

"For birth control," he stated flatly, watching her cheeks color. "I'll take care of it for now. But when we get back from our honeymoon, you make an appointment. I don't care what you choose, but I want you protected."

She felt as if he'd knocked her down and jumped on her feetfirst. "You know a lot about birth control for a bachelor," she faltered.

"That's why I'm still a bachelor," he replied coldly. He searched her eyes. "Children will be a mutual decision, not yours alone. I hope we've clarified that."

"You certainly have," she said.

"I'll see you at the church tomorrow." His eyes went over her quickly. "Try to get a good night's sleep. We've got a long day and a long trip ahead of us."

"Yes, I will."

He touched her hair, but he didn't kiss her. He laughed again, as if at some cold personal joke. He left her in the hallway without a backward glance. It was a foreboding sort of farewell for a couple on the eve of their wedding, and because of it, Tiffany didn't sleep at all.

Chapter Seven

The next day dawned with pouring rain. It was a gloomy morning that made Tiffany even more depressed than she had been to start with. She stared at her reflection in the mirror and hardly recognized herself. She didn't feel like the old devil-may-care Tiffany who would dare anything to get what she wanted from life. And she remembered with chilling precision the words of an old saying: *Be careful what you wish for; you might get it.*

She made up her face carefully, camouflaging her paleness and the shadows under her eyes. She dressed in her neat white suit and remembered belatedly that she hadn't thought to get a bouquet for the occasion. It was too late now. She put on her hat and pulled the thin veil over her eyes, picked up her purse, and went out to join her father in the downstairs hall. The house seemed empty and unnaturally quiet, and she wondered what her late mother would have thought of this wedding.

Harrison, in an expensive dark suit with a white rose in his lapel, turned and smiled at his daughter as she came down the staircase.

"You look lovely," he said. "Your mother would have been proud."

"I hope so."

He came closer, frowning as he took her hands and found them ice-cold. "Darling, are you sure this is what you want?" he asked solemnly. "It's not too late to call it off, you know, even now."

For one mad instant, she thought about it. Panic had set in firmly. But she'd gone too far.

"It will work out," she said doggedly, and smiled at her father. "Don't worry."

He sighed impotently and shrugged. "I can't help it. Neither of you looked much like a happy couple over dinner last night. You seemed more like people who'd just won a chance on the guillotine."

"Oh, Dad," she moaned, and then burst out laughing. "Trust you to come up with something outrageous!"

He smiled, too. "That's better. You had a ghostly pallor when you came down the stairs. We wouldn't want people to mistake this ceremony for a wake."

"God forbid!" She took his arm. "Well," she said, taking a steadying breath, "let's get it over with."

"Comments like that are so reassuring," he muttered to himself as he escorted her out the door and into the white limousine that was to take them to the small church.

Surprisingly, the parking lot was full of cars when they pulled up at the curb.

"I don't remember inviting anyone," she ventured.

"King probably felt obliged to invite his company people," he reminded her. "Especially his executive staff."

"Well, yes, I suppose so." She waited for the chauffeur to open the door, and she got out gingerly, keenly aware that she didn't have a bouquet. She left her purse in the limo, in which she and King would be leaving for the airport immediately after the service. A reception hadn't been possible in the time allocated. King would probably have arranged some sort of refreshments for his office staff, of course, perhaps at a local restaurant.

Tiffany entered the church on her father's arm, and they paused to greet two of King's vice presidents, whom they knew quite well.

King was standing at the altar with the minister. The decorations were unsettling. Instead of the bower of roses she'd hoped for, she found two small and rather scruffy-looking flower arrangements gracing both sides of the altar. Carelessly tied white ribbons festooned the front pews. Family would have been sitting there, if she and King had any close relatives. Neither did, although Tiffany claimed Lettie as family, and sure enough, there she sat, in a suit, and especially a hat, that would have made fashion headlines. Tiffany smiled involuntarily at the picture her fashionable godmother made. Good thing the newspapers weren't represented, she thought, or Lettie would have overshadowed the bride and groom for splendor in that exquisite silk dress. And, of course, the hat.

The minister spotted Tiffany in the back of the church with her father and nodded to the organist who'd been hired to provide music. The familiar strains of the "Wedding March" filled the small church.

Tiffany's knees shook as she and her father made their way down the aisle. She wondered how many couples had walked this aisle, in love and with hope and joy? God knew, she was scared to death of what lay ahead.

And just when she thought she couldn't feel any worse, she spotted Carla in the front pew on King's side of the church. With disbelief, she registered that the woman was wearing a white lacy dress with a white veiled hat! As if she, not Tiffany, were the bride!

She felt her father tense as his own gaze followed hers, but neither of them were unconventional enough to make any public scene. It was unbelievable that King would invite his paramour here, to his wedding. But, then, perhaps he was making a statement. Tiffany would be his wife, but he was making no concessions in his personal life. When confronted by the pitiful floral accessories, and her lack of a bouquet, she wasn't particularly surprised that he'd invited Carla. She and her dress were the final indignity of the day.

King glanced sideways as she joined him, her father relinquishing her and going quickly to his own seat. King's eyes narrowed on her trim suit and the absence of a bouquet. He scowled.

She didn't react. She simply looked at the minister and gave him all her attention as he began the ceremony.

There was a flutter when, near the end of the service, he called for King to put the ring on Tiffany's finger. King searched his pockets, scowling fiercely, until he found it loose in his slacks' pocket, where he'd placed it earlier. He slid it onto Tiffany's finger, his face hardening when he registered how cold her hand was.

The minister finished his service, asked if the couple had any special thing they'd like to say as part of the ceremony. When they looked uneasy, he quickly pronounced them man and wife and smiled as he invited King to kiss the bride.

King turned to his new wife and stared at her with narrowed eyes for a long moment before he pulled up the thin veil and bent to kiss her carelessly with cold, firm lips.

People from the front pews surged forward to offer congratulations. Lettie was first. She hugged Tiffany warmly, acting like a mother hen. Tiffany had to fight tears, because her new status would take her away from the only surrogate mother she'd ever known. But she forced a watery smile and started to turn to her father when she saw a laughing Carla lift her arms around King's neck and kiss him passionately, full on the mouth.

The minister looked as surprised as Tiffany and her father did. Harrison actually started forward, when Lettie took his arm.

"Walk me to my car, Harrison," Lettie directed.

Seconds later, King extricated himself and shook hands with several of his executives. Tiffany gave Carla a look that could have fried an egg and deliberately took her father's free arm.

"Shall we go?" she said to her two elderly companions.

"Really, dear, this is most...unconventional," Lettie faltered as Tiffany marched them out of the church.

"Not half as unconventional as forgetting which woman you married," she said loudly enough for King, and the rest of the onlookers, to hear her.

She didn't look at him, although she could feel furious eyes stabbing her in the back.

She didn't care. He and his lover had humiliated her beyond bearing, and on her wedding day. She was tempted to go home with her father and get an annulment on the spot.

As she stood near the limousine with Harrison and Lettie, debating her next move, King caught her arm and parceled her unceremoniously into the limousine. She barely had time to wave as the driver took off.

"That was a faux pas of the highest order," he snapped at her.

"Try saying that with less lipstick on your mouth, darling," she drawled with pure poison.

He dug for a handkerchief and wiped his mouth, coming away with the vivid orange shade that Carla had been wearing.

"My own wedding," she said in a choked tone, her hands mangling her small purse, "and you and that...creature...make a spectacle of the whole thing!"

"You didn't help," he told her hotly, "showing up in a suit, without even a bouquet."

"The bouquet should have come from you," she said with shredded pride. "I wasn't going to beg for one. Judging by those flower arrangements you provided, if you'd ordered a bouquet for me, it would have come with dandelions and stinging nettle! As for the suit, you didn't want a big wedding, and a fancy gown would have been highly inappropriate for such a small ceremony."

He laughed coldly, glaring at her. "You didn't say you wanted a bouquet."

"You can give Carla one later and save her the trouble of having to catch mine."

He cursed roundly.

"Go ahead," she invited. "Ruin the rest of the day."

"This whole damned thing was your idea," he snapped at her, tugging roughly at his constricting tie. "Marriage was never in my mind, until you started throwing yourself at me! God knew, an affair was never an option.''

She searched his averted profile sadly. As she'd feared, this had been, in many ways, a shotgun wedding. She mourned for the old days, when they were friends and enjoyed each other's company. Those days were gone forever.

''Yes. I know,'' she said heavily. She leaned back against the seat and felt as if she'd been dragged behind the car. She'd lost her temper, but it wasn't really his fault. He was as much a victim as she was, at the moment. ''I don't know why I should have expected you to jump with joy,'' she said when she'd calmed a little. ''You're right. I did force you into a marriage you didn't want. You have every right to be furious.'' She turned to him with dead eyes in a face like rice paper. ''There's no need to go on with this farce. We can get an annulment, right now. If you'll just have the driver take me home, I'll start it right away.''

He stared at her as if he feared for her sanity. ''Are you out of your mind?'' he asked shortly. ''We've just been married. What the hell do you think it will say to my executives and my stockholders if I annul my marriage an hour after the ceremony?''

''No one has to know when it's done,'' she said reasonably. ''You can fly to Jamaica and I'll go back to New York with Lettie until this all blows over.''

''Back to modeling, I suppose?'' he asked curtly.

She shrugged. ''It's something to do,'' she said.

"You have something to do," he returned angrily. "You're my wife."

"Am I?" she asked. "Not one person in that church would have thought so, after you kissed Carla. In fact, I must say, her dress was much more appropriate than mine for the occasion, right down to the veil."

He averted his eyes, almost as if he were embarrassed. She leaned back again and closed her own eyes, to shut him out.

"I don't care," she said wearily. "Decide what you want, and I'll do it. Anything at all, except," she added, turning her head to stare at him with cold eyes, "sleep with you. That I will not do. Not now."

His eyebrows arched. "What the hell do you mean?"

"Exactly what I just said," she replied firmly. "You can get...that...from Carla, with my blessings." She almost bit through her lip telling the flat lie. Pride was very expensive. She closed her eyes again, to hide the fear that he might take her up on it. "I've been living in a fool's paradise, looking for happily ever after, dreaming of satin and lace and delicious nights and babies. And all I've got to show for it is a secondhand lust without even the gloss of friendship behind it and an absolute edict that I'm never to think of having a child."

He sat back in his own seat and stared straight ahead. Yes, he'd said that. He'd been emphatic, in fact, about not having children right away. He'd withdrawn from her in the past two weeks, so deliberately that he'd given the impression of a man being forced to do something he abhorred. He'd arranged a quick ceremony, but he hadn't let his secretary—Carla—arrange the flowers. He'd left that duty to another subordinate. He wondered what the hell had gone wrong. Only two sparse and not-very-attractive flower arrangements had graced the church and Tiffany had been denied a bouquet. He knew that it was deliberate, that Carla was somehow involved, but there was no way to undo the damage. By the time he saw the flowers it was far too late to do anything. Carla's dress and the kiss had been as much a surprise to him as it had to Tiffany. She wouldn't believe it, though. She was thinking of the things he'd denied her.

She'd been denied more than just flowers, at that. She hadn't had a photographer, a ring bearer, flower girls and attendants, a reception—she'd lacked all those as well. And to top it all off, it looked as if he'd wanted to kiss his secretary instead of his new bride, in front of the whole assembly.

His eyes sought her averted face again, with bitter regret. He'd fought marrying her from the start, hating his weakness for her, punishing her for it. This had been a travesty of a wedding, all around. She was bitter and wounded, and it was his fault. He studied her drawn countenance with haunted eyes. He remembered Tiffany all aglitter with happiness and the sheer joy of living, teasing him, laughing with him, tempting him, loving him. He could have had all that, just for himself. But he'd let his fears and misgivings cloud the occasion, and Tiffany had suffered for them.

He drew in a long breath and turned his eyes back to the window. This, he thought wearily, was going to be some honeymoon.

In fact, it was some honeymoon, but not at all the sort Tiffany had once dreamed about having. Montego Bay was full of life, a colorful and fascinating place with a long history and the friendliest, most welcoming people Tiffany could ever remember in her life.

They had a suite at an expensive resort on the beach, and fortunately it contained two rooms. She didn't ask King what he thought of her decision to sleep in the smaller of the two rooms; she simply moved in. She paid him the same attention she'd have paid a female roommate, and she didn't care what he thought about that, either. It was her honeymoon. She'd had no real wedding, but she was going to have a honeymoon, even if she had to spend it alone.

King had brought along his laptop with its built-in fax-modem, and he spent the evening working at the small desk near the window.

Tiffany put on a neat beige trouser suit and fixed her hair in a soft bun atop her head. She didn't even worry with makeup.

"I'm going to the restaurant to have supper," she announced.

He looked up from his monitor, with quiet, strangely subdued eyes. "Do you want company?"

"Not particularly, thanks." She went out the door while he was getting used to being an unwelcome tourist.

She sat alone at a table and ate a seafood salad. She had a piña colada with her meal, and the amount of rum it contained sent her head spinning.

She was very happy, all of a sudden, and when a steel band began to play to the audience, she joined in the fun, clapping and laughing with the crowd.

It wasn't until a tall, swarthy man tried to pick her up that she realized how her behavior might be misinterpreted. She held up her left hand and gave the man a smile that held just the right portions of gratitude and regret. He bowed, nonplussed, and she got up to pay her bill.

King was out on the patio when she returned, but he looked at her curiously when she stumbled just inside the closed door and giggled.

"What the hell have you been doing?" he asked.

"Getting soused, apparently," she said with a vacant smile. "Do you have any idea how much rum they put in those drinks?"

"You never did have a head for hard liquor," he remarked with a faint smile.

"A man tried to pick me up."

The smile turned into a cold scowl. He came back into the room slowly. He'd changed into white slacks and a patterned silk shirt, which was hanging open over his dark-haired chest. He looked rakish with his hair on his forehead and his eyes glittering at her.

"I showed him my wedding ring," she said to placate him. "And I didn't kiss him. It is, after all, my wedding day."

"A hell of a wedding day," he replied honestly.

"If I hadn't gone all mushy, we'd still be friends," she said with a sad little sigh as the liquor made her honest. "I wish we were."

He moved a little closer and his chest rose and fell roughly. "So do I," he admitted tersely. He searched her sad eyes. "Tiffany, I...didn't want to be married."

"I know. It's all right," she said consolingly. "You don't have to be. When we get back, I'll go and see an attorney."

He didn't relax. His eyes were steady and curious, searching over her slender body, seeking out all the soft curves and lines of her. "You shouldn't have grown up."

"I didn't have much choice." She smothered a yawn and turned away. "Good night, King."

He watched her go with an ache in his belly that wouldn't quit. He wanted her, desperately. But an annulment would be impossible if he followed her into her room. And she'd already said that she didn't want him. He turned back to the cool breeze on the patio and walked outside, letting the wind cool his hot skin. He'd never felt so restless, or so cold inside.

* * *

Tiffany awoke with a blinding headache and nausea thick in her throat. She managed to sit up on the side of the bed in her simple white cotton gown. It covered every inch of her, and she was glad now that she'd decided not to pack anything suggestive or glamorous. She looked very young in the gown and without her makeup, with her dark hair in a tangle around her pale face.

King knocked at the door and then walked in, hesitating in the doorway with an expression of faint surprise when he saw the way she looked. His brows drew together emphatically.

"Are you all right?" he asked curtly.

"I have a hangover," she replied without looking at him. "I want to die."

He breathed roughly. "Next time, leave the rum to the experts and have a soft drink. I've got some tablets in my case that will help. I'll bring you a couple. Want some coffee?"

"Black, please," she said. She didn't move. Her head was splitting.

When he came back, she still hadn't stirred. He shook two tablets into her hand and gave her a glass of water to swallow them with. She thanked him and gave back the glass.

"I'll bring the coffee in as soon as room service gets here," he said. "I don't suppose you want breakfast, but it would help not to have an empty stomach."

"I can't eat anything." She eased back down on

the bed, curled up like a child with her eyes closed and a pillow shoved over her aching head.

He left her against his better judgment. A caring husband would have stayed with her, held her hand, offered sympathy. He'd fouled up so much for her in the past few weeks that he didn't think any overtures from him would be welcomed. She didn't even have to tell him why she'd had so much to drink the night before. He already knew.

Minutes later, he entered the room with the coffee and found Tiffany on the floor, gasping for breath. She couldn't seem to breathe. Her face was swollen. Red-rimmed eyes looked up at him with genuine panic.

"Good God." He went to the phone by her bed and called for a doctor, in tones that made threats if one wasn't forthcoming. Then he sat on the floor beside her, his expression one of subdued horror, trying to reassure her without a single idea what to do. She looked as if she might suffocate to death any minute.

The quick arrival of the doctor relieved his worry, but not for long.

Without even looking at King, the doctor jerked up the telephone and called for an ambulance.

"What did she eat?" the doctor shot at him as he filled a syringe from a small vial.

"Nothing this morning. She had a hangover. I gave her a couple of aspirins a few minutes ago..."

"Is she allergic to aspirin?" he asked curtly.

"I...don't know."

The doctor gave him a look that contained equal parts of contempt and anger. "You are her husband?" he asked with veiled sarcasm, then turned back to put the needle directly into the vein at her elbow.

"What are you giving her?" King asked curtly.

"Something to counteract an allergic reaction. You'd better go out and direct the ambulance men in here. Tell them not to lag behind."

King didn't argue, for once. He did exactly as he was told, cold all over as he took one last, fearful glance at Tiffany's poor swollen face. Her eyes were closed and she was still gasping audibly.

"Will she die?" King choked.

The doctor was counting her pulse. "Not if I can help it," he said tersely. "Hurry, man!"

King went out to the balcony and watched. He heard the ambulance arrive an eternity of seconds later. Almost at once ambulance attendants came into view. He motioned them up the stairs and into Tiffany's bedroom.

They loaded her onto a gurney and carried her out. Her color was a little better and she was breathing much more easily, but she was apparently unconscious.

"You can ride in the ambulance with her, if you like," the doctor invited.

King hesitated, not because he didn't want to go with her, but because he'd never been in such a position before and he was stunned.

"Follow in a cab, then," the other man rapped. "I'll ride with her."

He muttered under his breath, grabbed his wallet and key, locked the door, and went down to catch a cab at the front of the hotel. It was a simple exercise, there was always a cab waiting and a doorman to summon it.

Minutes later, he was pacing outside the emergency room waiting for the doctor to come out. Strange how quickly his priorities had changed and rearranged in the past few minutes. All it had taken was seeing Tiffany like that. He knew that as long as he lived, the sight of her on the floor would come back to haunt him. It had been so unnecessary. He'd never bothered to ask if she was allergic to anything. He hadn't wanted to know her in any intimate or personal way.

Now he realized that he knew nothing at all, and that his ignorance had almost cost her her life this morning. Nothing was as important now as seeing that she had the best care, that she got better, that she never had to suffer again because of a lack of interest or caring on his part. He might not have wanted this marriage, but divorce was not feasible. He had to make the best of it. And he would.

Chapter Eight

But the thing that hadn't occurred to him was that Tiffany might not care one way or the other for his concern. When she was released from the hospital later that day, with a warning not to ever touch aspirin again in any form, her whole attitude toward her husband had changed. Every ounce of spirit seemed to have been drained out of her.

She was quiet, unusually withdrawn on the way back to the hotel in the taxi. Her paleness hadn't abated, despite her treatment. The swelling had gone, but she was weak. He had to help her from the taxi and into the hotel.

"I never asked if you had allergies," King said as he supported her into the elevator. He pushed the button for their floor. "I'm sorry this happened."

"The whole thing was my fault," she said wearily. "My head hurt so bad that it never occurred to me to question what you were giving me. I haven't had an aspirin since I was thirteen.''

He studied her as she leaned back against the wall of the elevator, looking as if she might collapse any minute. ''One way or another, you've had a hell of a wedding.''

She laughed mirthlessly. ''Yes, I have.''

The elevator jerked to a stop and the doors opened. King abruptly swung her up into his arms and carried her to their room, putting her down only long enough to produce the key and open the door.

She let her head rest on his broad shoulder and closed her eyes, pretending that he loved her, pretending that he wanted her. She'd lived on dreams of him most of her life, but reality had been a staggering blow to her pride and her heart. They were married, and yet not married.

He carried her into the sitting room and deposited her gently on the sofa. ''Are you hungry?'' he asked. ''Do you think you could eat something?''

''A cold salad, perhaps,'' she murmured. ''With thousand island dressing, and a glass of milk.''

He phoned room service, ordering that for her and a steak and salad and a beer for himself.

''I didn't know you ever drank beer,'' she mused when he hung up.

He glanced at her curiously. ''We've lived in each other's pockets for as long as I can remember,'' he said. ''Amazing, isn't it, how little we actually know about each other.''

She pushed back her disheveled hair with a sigh

and closed her eyes. "I don't think there's a drop of anything left in my poor stomach. I couldn't eat last night. I didn't even have breakfast this morning."

"And you don't need to lose weight," he stated solemnly. He scowled as he searched over her body. "Tiffany, you've dropped a few pounds lately."

"I haven't had much appetite for several months," she said honestly. "It wasn't encouraged when I was modeling. After I came home, and we...decided to get married, I was too busy to eat a lot. It's been a hectic few weeks."

He hadn't missed the hesitation when she spoke of their decision to marry. He hated the way she looked. The change in her was so dramatic that anyone who'd known her even a year before wouldn't recognize her.

His heavy sigh caught her attention.

"Do you want to go home?" she asked.

The sadness in her eyes hurt him. "Only if you do," he said. "There are plenty of things to see around here. We could go up and walk around Rose Hall, for example," he added, mentioning a well-known historical spot.

But she shook her head. "I don't feel like sightseeing, King," she told him honestly. "Couldn't we go home?"

He hesitated. She was worn-out from the rushed wedding, the trip over here, her experience with the allergic reaction. He wanted to tell her that a night's sleep might make all the difference, but the sight of her face was enough to convince him that she'd do better in her own environment.

"All right," he said gently. "If that's what you want. We'll leave at the end of the week. I'll try to get tickets first thing in the morning."

She nodded. "Thank you."

Room service came with their orders and they ate in a strained silence. Tiffany finished her salad and coffee and then, pleading tiredness, got up to go to bed.

She started for her own room.

"Tiffany."

His deep voice stopped her at the doorway. She turned. "Yes?"

"Sleep with me."

Her heart jerked in her chest. Her eyes widened.

"No," he said, shaking his head as he got to his feet. "I don't want you that way yet, honey," he said softly, to lessen the blow of the statement. "You don't need to be alone tonight. It's a king-size bed, and you won't need to worry that I'll take advantage."

It was very tempting. He'd hardly touched her in almost a month. And although he didn't know it, any fear of having him take advantage of the situation was nonexistent. She sometimes felt that she'd have given six months of her life to have him throw her down onto the nearest available surface and ravish her to the point of exhaustion. She wondered what he'd say if she admitted that. Probably it would be just one more complication he didn't want. And there was still Carla, waiting back home.

"All right," she said after a minute. "If you don't mind…"

"Mind!" He bit off the word and turned away before she could see his strained face. "No," he said finally. "I don't…mind."

He was behaving very oddly, she mused as she showered and then put on another of her white embroidered gowns. The garment was very concealing and virginal, and there was a cotton robe that matched it, with colorful pastel embroidery on the collar and the hem, and even on the belt that secured it around her trim waist.

When she walked into the other room and approached King's, through the slightly open door she heard him talking on the telephone.

"…be home tomorrow," he was saying. "I'll want everything ready when I get to the office. Yes, we'll talk about that," he added in a cold, biting tone. "No, I wouldn't make any bets on it. You do that. And don't foul things up this time or it will be the last mistake you make on my payroll. Is that clear?"

He put down the receiver with an angry breath and ran a hand through his own damp hair. He was wearing an incredibly sexy black velour robe with silver trim. When he turned, Tiffany's knees went weak at the wide swath of hair-roughened chest it bared to her hungry eyes.

He was looking at her, too. The gown and robe

should have been dampening to any man's ardor, because she looked as virginal as he knew she was. But it inflamed him. With her face soft in the lamplight, her eyes downcast, she made him ache.

"Which side of the bed do you want?" he asked curtly.

"I like the left, but it doesn't matter."

He waved her toward it. Trying not to notice that he was watching her obsessively, she drew off the robe and spread it across the back of a nearby chair before she turned down the covers and, tossing off her slippers, climbed under the sheet.

He looked at her with darkening, narrowed eyes. She could see his heartbeat, it was so heavy. While she watched, his hand went to the loop that secured the belt of his robe and loosened it, catching the robe over one arm to toss it aside. He stood there, completely nude, completely aroused, and let her look.

Her lips parted. It was a blatant, arrogant action. She didn't know what to do or say. She couldn't manage words. He was…exquisite. He had a body that would have made the most jaded woman swoon with pleasure. And, remembering the heated mastery of his lovemaking, her body throbbed all over. It was in her eyes, her flushed face, her shaking heartbeat.

"Take it off," he said in a husky soft tone. "I want to look at you."

She wasn't able to think anymore. She clammered out from under the sheet and onto her knees, struggling to throw off the yards of concealing cotton. At last, she tugged it over her head and threw it onto the floor. Her body was as aroused as his. He knew the signs.

He moved around the bed. As he came closer, he caught the rose scent of her. Forgotten was the rocky start to their honeymoon, the accusations, the sudden illness. He approached her like a predator.

She made a helpless little sound and abruptly reached beside her to sweep both pillows off the bed and onto the floor as she surged backward, flat on the sheet, her legs parted, her arms beside her head. She trembled there, waiting, a little afraid of the overwhelming masculinity of him, but hungry and welcoming despite it.

He came onto the bed, slowly, stealthily, as if he still expected her to bolt. One lean, powerful leg inserted itself between both of hers, his chest hovered above hers, his arms slid beside her, his fingers interlaced with her own and pinned them beside her ears.

"It's…pagan." She choked.

He understood. He nodded slowly, and still his eyes held hers, unblinking, as his leg moved against the inside of hers in a sinuous, sensual touch that echoed the predatory approach of his mouth to her parted lips.

It was like fencing, she thought half-dazed. His body teased her, his mouth teased her, every part of him was an instrument of seduction. It was nothing like their earlier lovemaking, when he'd kissed her, touched her, even pleasured her. This was the real thing, a prowling, tenderly violent stalking of the female by the male, a controlled savagery of pleasure that enticed but never satisfied, that aroused and denied all at the same time.

Her body shook as if with a fever and she arched, pleaded, pulled, twisted, trying to make him end it. The tension was at a level far beyond any that he'd ever subjected her to.

He touched her very briefly and then, finally—finally!—moved down into the intimacy that she'd begged for. But even as it came, it frightened her. She stiffened, her nails digging into his muscular arms, her teeth biting at her lower lip.

He stilled. His heart was beating furiously, but his eyes, despite their fierce need, were tender.

"First times are always difficult," he whispered. He held her eyes as he moved again, very gently. "Can you feel me, there?" he murmured wickedly, bending to brush his smiling lips against hers. They rested there as he moved again. "Talk to me."

"*Talk?*" She gasped as she felt him invading her. "Good...Lord...!"

"Talk to me," he chided, laughing as she clutched him. "This isn't a ritual of silence. We're learning each other in the most intimate way there is. It shouldn't be an ordeal. Look down my body while I'm taking you. See how it looks when we fit together like puzzle pieces."

"I couldn't!" she gasped.

"Why?" He stilled and deliberately lifted himself for a few seconds. "Look, Tiffany," he coaxed. "It isn't frightening, or sordid, or ugly. We're becoming lovers. It's the most beautiful thing a man and woman can share, especially when it's as emotional as it is physical. Look at us.''

It was a powerful enticement, and it worked. But her shocked eyes didn't linger. They went quickly back to his, as if to seek comfort and reassurance.

''You're my wife,'' he whispered softly. He caught his breath as his next movement took him completely to the heart of her, and his eyes closed and he shivered.

Seeing him vulnerable like that seemed to rob her of fear and the slight discomfort of their intimate position. One of her hands freed itself and moved hesitantly to touch his drawn face, to sift through his thick, cool black hair. His eyes opened, as if the caress startled him.

It was incredible, to look at him and talk to him with the lights on while they fused in the most shocking way. But he didn't seem at all shocked. In fact, he watched her the whole time. When his hips began to move lazily against hers and the shock of pleasure lifted her tight against him, and she gasped, he actually laughed.

''For...shame!'' She choked, shivering with each movement as unexpected pleasure rippled through her.

''Why?'' he taunted.

''You laughed!''

''You delight me,'' he whispered, bending to nibble her lips as his movements lengthened and deepened. "I've never enjoyed it like this."

Which was an uncomfortable reminder that he was no novice. She started to speak, but as if he sensed what she was going to say, he suddenly shifted and she was overwhelmed by the most staggering pleasure she'd ever felt.

It possessed her. She couldn't even breathe. She arched up, helpless, her mouth open, her eyes dazed, gasping with each deliberate movement of his body. She was trying to grasp something elusive and explosive, reaching toward it with every thread of her being. It was just out of her reach, almost, almost, tantalizingly close...

"Oh...please!" she managed to say in a shuddering little cry.

He looked somber, almost violent in that instant. He said something, but she didn't hear him. Just as the tension abruptly snapped and she heard her own voice sobbing in unbearable pleasure, his face buried itself in her soft throat and his own body shuddered with the same sweet anguish.

For a long time afterward, his breathing was audible, raspy and unsteady at her ear. She gasped for air, but she was still clinging to him, as if she could retain just a fragment of that extraordinary wave of pleasure that had drowned her for endless seconds.

"It doesn't last," she whispered shakenly.

"It couldn't," he replied heavily. "The human body can only bear so much of it without dying."

Her hands spread on his damp shoulders with a

sort of wonder at the feel of him so deep in her body. She moved her hips and felt the pleasure ripple through her unexpectedly.

She laughed at her discovery.

He lifted his dark head and his eyes, sated now, searched hers. "Experimenting?"

She nodded, and moved gently again, gasping as she found what she was searching for. But along with it came a new and unfamiliar stinging sensation and she stilled.

He brushed back her damp hair gently. "Your body has to get used to this," he murmured. "Right now, you need rest more than you need me." He moved very slowly and balanced himself on his hands. "Try to relax," he whispered. "This may be uncomfortable."

Which was an understatement. She closed her eyes and ground her teeth together as he lifted away from her.

He eased over onto his back with a heavy breath and turned his head toward her. "And now you know a few things that you didn't, before," he mused, watching her expressions. "Want a bath or just a wet cloth?"

The matter-of-fact question shouldn't have shocked her, but it did. Her nudity shocked her, too, and so did his. Without the anesthetic of passion, sex was very embarrassing. She got to her feet and gathered up her gown, holding it over her front.

"I...I think I'd like a shower," she stammered.

He got out of bed, completely uninhibited, and

took the gown from her fingers, tossing it onto the bed. "None of that," he taunted softly. "We're an old married couple now. That means we can bathe together."

Her expression was complicated. "We can?"

"We can."

He led her into the bathroom, turned on the shower jets, and plopped her in before him.

It was an adventure to bathe with someone. She was alternately embarrassed, intrigued, amused, and scandalized by it. But she laughed with pure delight at this unexpected facet of married life. It had never occurred to her that she might take a shower with King, even in her most erotic dreams.

Afterward, they dried each other and he carried her back to bed, placing her neatly under the covers, nude, before he joined her and turned off the lights.

He caught her wandering hand and drew it to his hairy chest with a chuckle.

"Stop that," he murmured. "You're used up. No more for you tonight, or probably tomorrow, either."

She knew he was right, but she was still bristling with curiosity and the newness of intimacy.

His hand smoothed her soft hair. "We have years of this ahead of us," he reminded her quietly. "You don't have to rush in as if tonight was the last night we'd ever have together."

She lay against him without speaking. That was how it had felt, though. There was a sort of desperation in it, a furious seeking and holding. She didn't

understand her own fears, except that she was fatally
uncertain of Kingman Marshall's staying power.
Carla still loomed in the background, and even if
he'd found Tiffany enjoyable in bed, he was still
getting used to a married status that he'd never
wanted. She didn't kid herself that it was smooth
sailing from now on. In fact, the intimacy they'd just
shared might prove to be more of a detriment than
an advantage in the cold light of day.

The worry slowly drifted away, though, as she lay
in her husband's warm arms and inhaled the expensive scent of his cologne. Tomorrow would come,
but for tonight, she could pretend that she was a
much-loved wife with a long happy marriage ahead
of her. King must know that she hadn't had time to
see a doctor about any sort of birth control. But he
apparently hadn't taken care of it as he'd said he
would. He'd been too hungry for her to take time to
manage it himself.

She thought of a child and her whole body
warmed and flushed. He didn't want children, but
she did, desperately. If he did leave her for Carla,
she'd have a small part of him that the other woman
could never take from her.

From pipe dreams to reality was a hard fall. But
she woke alone the next day, with her gown tossed
haphazardly on the bed with her. King was nowhere
in sight, and it was one o'clock in the afternoon!

She put on the gown and her slippers and robe
and padded slowly out into the sitting room of the

suite. It was empty, too. Perturbed, she went across into her own room and found some white jeans and a red-and-blue-and-white jersey to slip into. She tied her hair back in a red ribbon, slipped on her sneakers, and started to go out and look for King when she saw the envelope on the dresser.

Her name was on the front in a familiar bold black slash. She picked up the envelope and held it, savoring for a moment the night before, because she knew inside herself that whatever was in that envelope was going to upset her.

She drew out a piece of hotel stationery and unfolded it.

Tiffany,
I've left your passport, and money for a return ticket and anything else you need in your purse. I've paid the hotel bill. An emergency came up back home. I meant to tell you last night that I had to leave first thing this morning, but it slipped my mind. I managed to get the last seat on a plane to San Antonio. We'll talk later.
King.

She read it twice more, folded it, and put it into the envelope. What sort of emergency was so pressing that a man had to leave his honeymoon to take care of it?

That was when something niggled at the back of her mind, and she remembered the snatch of conversation she'd overheard before they'd gone to bed.

King had said that he'd be home tomorrow—today. She drew in a harsh breath. *Carla.* Carla had phoned him and he'd left his wife to rush home. She'd have bet her last dollar that there was no emergency at all, unless it was that he was missing his old lover. Apparently, she thought with despair, even the heated exchange of the night before hadn't been enough for him. And why should it? She was a novice, only a new experience for him. Carla was probably as expert as he was.

With wounded pride stiffening her backbone, she picked up the telephone and dialed the international code and her father's private office number.

"Hello?" he answered after a minute.

The sound of his voice was so dear and comforting that she hesitated a few seconds to choke back hurt tears. "Hi, Dad," she said.

"What the hell's going on?" he demanded. "King phoned me from the airport and said he was on his way into the city to sort out some union dispute at one of the branch offices. Since when do we have a union dispute?" he asked irritably.

"I don't know any more than you do," she said. "He left me a note."

He sighed angrily. "I could have dealt with a dispute, if there had been one. I've been doing it longer than he has, and I'm the senior partner."

He didn't have to say that. She already knew it. "I'm coming home tomorrow," she told him. "I, uh, sort of had a bout with some aspirin and I'm feeling bad. I was ready to leave, but there was only one seat available on the morning flight. We agreed that I'd follow tomorrow," she lied glibly.

It sounded fishy to Harrison, but he didn't say a word about it. "You're allergic to aspirin," he said pointedly.

"I know, but King didn't. I had a splitting headache and he gave me some. He had to take me to the hospital, but I'm fine now, and he knows not to give me aspirin again."

"Damnation!" her father growled. "Doesn't he know anything about you?"

"Oh, he's learning all the time," she assured him. "I'll talk to you tomorrow, Dad. Can you have the car meet me at the airport? I'm not sure if King will remember me, if he's involved in meetings." *Or with Carla,* she thought. King hadn't said anything about her coming home at all in his terse little note. She was going to be a surprise.

There was an ominous pause. "I'll remember you. Phone me when you get in. Take care, darling."

"You, too, Dad. See you."

He put down the receiver, got out of his chair, and made the door in two strides. He went past his secretary and down the hall to King's office, pushed open the door on a startled Carla, and slammed it back.

She actually gasped. "Mr....Mr. Blair, can I do something for you?"

"You can stop trying to sabotage my daughter's marriage, you black-eyed little pit viper," he said with furious eyes. "First you fouled up the flowers, then you wore a dress to the ceremony that even to the most unprejudiced person in the world looked like a wedding gown. You kissed the groom as if you were the bride, and now you've managed to get King back here on some tom fool excuse, leaving his bride behind in Jamaica!"

Carla's eyes almost popped. "Mr. Blair, honestly, I never meant..."

"You're fired," he said furiously.

She managed to get to her feet and her cheeks flamed. "Mr. Blair, I'm King's secretary," she said through her teeth. "You can't fire me!"

"I own fifty-one percent of the stock," he told her with pure contempt. "That means I can fire whom I damned well please. I said, you're fired, and that means you're fired."

She drew an indignant breath. "I'll file a complaint," she snapped back.

"Go right ahead," he invited. "I'll call the tabloids and give them a story that you'll have years to live down, after they do a little checking into your background."

It was only a shot in the dark, but she didn't know that. Her face went paper white. She actually shivered.

"Your severance pay will be waiting for you on the way out," he said shortly.

He went out the office door, almost colliding with King.

"I've just fired your damned secretary!" Harrison

told King with uncharacteristic contempt. "And if you want a divorce from my daughter so you can go chasing after your sweet little paramour, here, I'll foot the bill! The two of you deserve each other!"

He shouldered past King and stormed away down the hall, back into his own office. The walls actually shook under the force with which he slammed the door.

King gave Carla a penetrating look. He walked into the office, and closed the door. Harrison had beaten him to the punch. He was going to fire Carla, but first he wanted some answers.

"All right," he said. "Let's have it."

"Have what?" she faltered. She moved close to him, using every wile she had for all she was worth. "You aren't going to let him fire me, are you?" she teased, moving her hips gently against his body. "Not after all we've been to one another?"

He stiffened, but not with desire, and stepped back. "What we had was over long before I married Tiffany."

"It never had to be," she cooed. "She's a child, a little princess. What can she be to a man like you? Nothing more than a new experience."

"You phoned and said there was a labor dispute," he reminded her. "I can't find a trace of it."

She shrugged. "Tom said there were rumors of a strike and that I'd better let you know. Ask him, if you don't believe me." She struck a seductive pose. "Are you going to let him fire me?" she asked again.

He let out a harsh breath. Harrison was breathing fire. Apparently he'd got the wrong end of the stick and Carla had done nothing to change his mind.

"You've made an enemy of him," King told her. "A bad one. Your behavior at the wedding is something he won't forget."

"You will," she said confidently. "You didn't want to marry her. You didn't even check about the flowers or a silly bouquet, because you didn't care, and she embarrassed you by wearing a suit to get married in." She made a moue of distaste. "It was a farce."

"Yes, thanks to you." He stuck his hands into his pockets and glowered at her. He wondered how far out of his mind he'd been to get involved with this smiling boa constrictor. She'd been exciting and challenging, but now she was a nuisance. "I'll see what I can do about getting you another job. But not here," he added quietly. "I'm not going against Harrison."

"Is that why you married her?" she asked. "So that you could be sure of inheriting the whole company when he dies?"

"Don't be absurd."

She shrugged. "Maybe it's why she married you, too," she said, planting a seed of doubt. "She'll have security now, even if you divorce her, won't she?"

Divorce. Harrison had said something about a divorce. "I have to talk to Harrison," he said shortly.

"You'll work your two weeks notice, despite what he said, and I'll see what's going at another office."

"Thank you, sweet," she murmured. She moved close and reached up to kiss him. "You're a prince!"

He went out the door with a handkerchief to his mouth, wiping off the taste of her on his way to his partner's office.

Chapter Nine

Harrison just glared at King when he went into the office and closed the door behind him.

"I don't care what you say, she's history," Harrison told the younger man. "She's meddled in my daughter's affairs for the last time!"

King scowled. He didn't like the look of his partner. "I haven't said a word," he said softly. "Calm down. If you want her to go, she goes. But let her work out her notice."

Harrison relaxed a little. His eyes were still flashing. He looked deathly pale and his breathing was unusually strained. He loosened his tie. "All right. But that's all. That silly woman," he said in a raspy voice. "She's caused...Tiffany...no end of heartache already, and now I've got...to cause her... more..." He paused with a hand to his throat and laughed in surprise. "That's funny. My throat hurts, right up to my jaw. I can't..." He grimaced and suddenly slumped to the floor. He looked gray and sweat covered his face.

King buzzed Harrison's secretary, told her to phone the emergency services number immediately and get some help into Harrison's office.

It was terribly apparent that Harrison was having a heart attack. His skin was cold and clammy and his lips were turning blue. King began CPR at once, and in no time, he had two other executives of the company standing by to relieve him, because he had no idea how long he'd have to keep it up before the ambulance came.

As it happened, less than five minutes elapsed between the call and the advent of two EMTs with a gurney. They got Harrison's heartbeat stabilized, hooked him up to oxygen and rushed him down to the ambulance with King right beside them.

"Any history of heart trouble in him or his family?" the EMT asked abruptly as he called the medical facility for orders.

"I don't know," King said irritably. For the second time in less than a week, he couldn't answer a simple question about the medical backgrounds of the two people he cared for most in the world. He felt impotent. "How's he doing?" he asked.

"He's stabilized, but these things are tricky," the EMT said. "Who's his personal physician?"

Finally, a question he could answer. He gave the information, which was passed on to the doctor answering the call at the medical center.

"Any family to notify?" the man relayed.

"I'm his son-in-law," King said grimly. "My wife is in Jamaica. I'll have to get her back here." He dreaded that. He'd have to tell her on the phone, and it was going to devastate her. But they couldn't afford the loss of time for him to fly down there after her. Harrison might not live that long.

The ambulance pulled up at the hospital, and Harrison, still unconscious, was taken inside to the emergency room. King went with him, pausing just long enough to speak with the physician before he found a pay phone and called the hotel in Jamaica. But more complications lay in store. Mrs. Marshall, he was told, had checked out that very morning. No, he didn't know where she'd gone, he was sorry.

King hung up, running an angry hand through his hair. Playing a grim hunch, he telephoned Harrison's house instead of his own. A maid answered the call.

"This is Kingman Marshall. Is my wife there?" he asked.

"Why, yes, sir. She got in about two hours ago. Shall I get her for you?"

He hesitated. "No. Thank you."

This was one thing he couldn't do on the phone. He told the doctor where he was going, hailed a taxi and had it drive him to Harrison's home.

Tiffany was upstairs, unpacking. She paled when she saw King come in the door. She hadn't expected her father to be at home, since it was a working day. She hadn't expected to see King, either.

"Looking for me?" she asked coolly. "I've decided that I'm going to live here until the divorce."

Divorce! Everything he was going to say went right out of his mind. He'd left her after the most exquisite loving of his life. Hadn't he explained the emergency that had taken him from her side? It wasn't as if he hadn't planned to fly right back. He'd had no idea at all that Carla had manufactured the emergency.

"Tiffany," he began, "I flew back because there was an emergency..."

"Yes, and I know what it was," she replied, having phoned the office just awhile ago. "My father fired your secretary, and you had to rush back to save her job. I've just heard all about it from the receptionist, thanks."

"The receptionist?"

"I wanted to know if you were in. She talked to someone and said I should call back, you were in the middle of some sort of argument with my father..."

He let out a short breath. "We'll talk about that later. There's no time. Your father's had a heart attack. He's in the emergency room at city general. Get your purse and let's go."

She grasped her bedpost. "Is he alive? Will he be all right?"

"He was seeing the doctor when I left to fetch you," he replied. "Come on."

She went out with him, numb and shocked and frightened to death. Her life was falling apart. How would she go on if she lost her father? He was the only human being on earth who loved her, who needed her, who cared about her.

Through waves of fear and apprehension, she sat motionless as he drove her Jaguar to the hospital. When he pulled up at the emergency entrance and stopped, she leapt out and ran for the doors, not even pausing to wait for him.

She went straight to the clerk, rudely pushing in front of the person sitting there.

"Please." She choked, "my father, Harrison Blair, they just brought him in with a heart attack…?"

The clerk looked very worried. "You need to speak with the doctor, Miss Blair. Just one minute…"

King joined her in time to hear the clerk use her maiden name. Under different circumstances, he'd have been furious about that. But this wasn't the time.

The clerk motioned Tiffany toward another door. King took her arm firmly and went with her, sensing calamity.

A white-coated young doctor gestured to them, but he didn't take them into the cubicle where King had left her father. Instead, he motioned them farther down the hall to a small cluster of unoccupied seats.

"I'm sorry. I haven't done much of this yet, and I'm going to be clumsy about it," the young man said solemnly. "I'm afraid we lost him. I'm very sorry. It was a massive heart attack. We did everything we possibly could. It wasn't enough.''

He patted her awkwardly on the upper arm, his face contorted with compassion.

''Thank you,'' King said quietly, and shook his hand. ''I'm sure it's hard for you to lose a patient.''

The doctor looked surprised, but he recovered quickly. ''We'll beat these things one day,'' he said gently. ''It's just that we don't have the technology yet. The worst thing is that his family physician told us he had no history of heart problems.'' He shook his head. ''This was unexpected, I'm sure. But it was quick, and painless, if that's any comfort.'' He looked at Tiffany's stiff, shocked face and then back at King. ''Bring her along with you, please. I'll give you something for her. She's going to need it. Any allergies to medicines?'' he asked at once.

''Aspirin,'' King said. He glanced down at Tiffany, subduing his own sorrow at Harrison's loss. ''Are you allergic to anything else, sweetheart?'' he added tenderly.

She shook her head. She didn't see, didn't hear, didn't think. Her father was dead. King had argued with him over Carla. Her father was dead because of King.

She pushed his hand away. Her eyes, filled with hatred, seared into his mind as she looked up at him. ''This is your fault.'' She choked. ''My father is dead! Was keeping Carla worth his life?''

He sucked in a sharp breath. ''Tiffany, that wasn't what happened…''

She moved away from him, toward the cubicle where the doctor was waiting. She was certain that she never wanted to speak to her husband again for as long as she lived.

The next few days were a total black void. There were the arrangements to be made, a service to arrange, minor details that somehow fell into place with King's help. The Blair home became like a great empty tomb. Lettie came to stay, of course, and King did, too, in spite of her protests. He slept in a bedroom down the hall from Tiffany's, watching her go through life in a trance while he dealt with friends and lawyers and the funeral home. She spoke to him only when it became necessary. He couldn't really blame her for the way she felt. She was too upset to reason. There would be plenty of time to explain things to her when she'd had time to recover. Meanwhile, Carla was on her way out of the office despite her plea to work out her notice. On that one point, King had been firm. She had her severance pay and a terse letter of recommendation. If only he could have foreseen, years ago, the trouble it was going to cause him when he put her out of his life, all this anguish with Tiffany might have been avoided. But at that time, Carla had been an exciting companion and he'd never considered marrying anyone. Now he was paying the price for his arrogance.

Undaunted by her firing, Carla showed up at the funeral home, only to be escorted right back out

again by King. She made some veiled threat about
going to the tabloids with her story, and he invited
her to do her worst. She was out of his life. Nothing
she did would ever matter to him again, and he said
so. She left, but with a dangerous glint in her cold
eyes.

She didn't come to the funeral service, Tiffany
noted, or to the graveside service. Apparently she'd
been told that it wasn't appropriate. Some people,
Lettie had said huffily, had no breeding and no sen-
sitivity. She said it deliberately, and within King's
hearing. He didn't react at all. Whatever he felt, he
was keeping it to himself.

The only chip in his stony front came the night
of the funeral, when he sat in Harrison's study with
only a lamp burning and downed a third of a bottle
of Harrison's fine Scotch whiskey.

Lettie intruded long enough to ask if he wanted
anything else from the kitchen before the housekeeper closed it up.

He lifted the glass toward her. "I'm drinking my
supper, thanks," he drawled.

Lettie closed the door behind her and paused in
front of the big antique oak desk, where his booted
feet were propped on its aged, pitted surface.

"What are you going to do about the house?"
she asked abruptly. Her eyes were red. She'd cried
for Harrison almost as much as Tiffany had. Now
her only concern was the girl's future.

"What do you mean, what am I going to do?" he asked. "It belongs to Tiffany."

"No, it doesn't," Lettie said worriedly. "Harrison was certain right up until the wedding ceremony that you weren't going to go through with the marriage. He wanted Tiffany provided for if something happened to him, and he didn't want her to have to be dependent on you. So he went to see his personal accountant about having everything he owned put in trust for her, including the house and his half of the business." She folded her hands at her waist, frowning worriedly. "But the accountant couldn't be located. Then Harrison found out that the man had been steadily embezzling from him for the past three years." She lifted her hands and spread them. "Just this week, he learned that a new mortgage had been taken out on the house and grounds and the money transferred to an account in a Bahamian bank." She grimaced as King lowered his feet to the floor and sat up. "He'd hired a private detective and was to see his attorney this afternoon after filing a lawsuit against the man before he skips the country with what's left of Harrison's fortune. If you can't stop him, Tiffany will be bankrupt."

"Good God!" King got to his feet, weaving a little. "No wonder he was so upset! Lettie, why the hell didn't you say something before this?"

"Because I wasn't sure that I had the right to involve you, except where the business is concerned," she said flatly. "You must know that Tiffany doesn't want to continue your marriage."

His face was drawn taut like a rope. "I know it."

She shrugged. "But there's no one else who can deal with this. I certainly can't. I can't even balance my checkbook. I wouldn't know how to proceed against the man."

King leaned forward with his head in his hands. "Get me a pot of strong coffee," he said through heavy breaths. "Then I want every scrap of information you have on the man and what Harrison planned."

Lettie brightened just a little. "We'll all miss him," she said gently as she turned toward the door. "But Tiffany most of all. He was both parents to her, for most of her life." She hesitated. "She needs you."

He didn't reply. She didn't seem to expect him to. She went out and closed the door behind her.

Tiffany was sitting on the bottom step of the staircase, looking pale and worn. Her eyes were red and she had a crumpled handkerchief in her hand. The long white gown and robe she was wearing seemed to emphasize her thinness.

"Child, you should be in bed," Lettie chided softly.

"I can't sleep." She stared at the study door. "Is he in there?"

Lettie nodded.

"What's he doing?"

"Getting drunk."

That was vaguely surprising. "Oh."

"I want to know why my father had a heart attack," she said grimly. "The receptionist wouldn't let me speak with King the day Daddy died because he and my father were arguing. Then at the funeral, one of his co-workers said it was a pity about the blow-up, because it was only seconds later when he collapsed. I know he fired Carla. Was that why King argued with him?"

"I don't know, Tiffany," she said, approaching the girl, "this is a vulnerable time for all of us. Don't say anything, do anything, that you'll have cause to regret later. King's hurt, too. He respected Harrison. Even if they did argue, they were friends as well as business partners for a long time."

"They were friends until I married King," Tiffany corrected her. "My father thought it was a mistake. He was right."

"Was he? It's early days yet, and some marriages can have a rocky beginning. It's no easy thing to make a life with another person. Fairy tales notwithstanding, even the most loving couples have to adjust to a shared coexistence."

"It helps if both partners work at it," Tiffany said.

"I agree. Get in there and do your part," her godmother prodded, jerking her red head toward the closed study door. "If you want answers, he's the only person who's got them."

Tiffany stared at the carpet for a minute and then got slowly to her feet.

"That's the idea," Lettie said. "I'm going to make him a pot of coffee. We have a few complications. Get him to tell you about them. Shared problems are another part of building a marriage.''

Tiffany laughed, but without mirth. She went to the door after Lettie vanished down the hall and opened it.

King glanced at her from behind the desk as she came into the room. ''I didn't plan to strand you in Montego Bay,'' he said pointedly. ''I would have been on my way back that night.''

''Would you?'' She went to the chair in front of the desk, a comfortable burgundy leather armchair that she'd occupied so many times when she and her father had talked. She sighed. ''The whole world has changed since then.''

''Yes. I know.''

She leaned back, sliding her hands over the cold leather arms, over the brass studs that secured it to the frame. ''Tell me how he died, King.''

He hesitated, but only for a second. His chiseled mouth tugged into a mocking smile. ''So they couldn't wait to tell you, hmm? I'm not surprised. Gossip loves a willing ear.''

''Nobody told me anything. It was inferred.''

''Same difference.'' He spread his hands on the desk and stood up. ''Okay, honey, you want the truth, here it is. He fired Carla and they had a royal row over it. I walked in and he started on me. I followed him to his office and got there just in time to watch him collapse.''

She let out the breath she'd been holding. Her nails bit into the leather arms of the chair. ''Why did you follow him? Were you going to talk him out of it?''

''No. But there's more to this than an argument over Carla,'' he added, searching for the right way to explain to her the tangled and devastating fact of her father's loss of wealth.

''Yes, there is. We've already agreed that I maneuvered you into a marriage you didn't want,'' she said curtly. ''We can agree that what happened in Montego Bay was a form of exorcism for both of us and let it go at that,'' she added when he started to speak. ''Charge me with desertion, mental cruelty, anything you like. Let me know when the papers are ready and I'll sign them.''

His eyes flashed like black fires. ''There won't be a divorce,'' he said shortly.

She was surprised by the vehemence in his tone, until she remembered belatedly just what her status was. As her father's heir, by a quirk of fate she was now his business partner. He couldn't afford to divorce her. What an irony.

She cocked her head and looked at him with cold curiosity. ''Oh, yes, I forgot, didn't I? We're business partners now. How nice to have it all in the family. You won't even have to buy me out. What's mine is yours.''

The look on his face was a revelation. Amazing how he could pretend that the thought had never occurred to him.

''That's a nice touch, that look of surprise,'' she

said admirably. "I expect you practiced in front of a mirror."

"Why are you downstairs at this hour of the night?" he asked.

"I couldn't sleep," she replied, and was suddenly vulnerable. She hated having it show. "My father was buried today," she drawled, "in case you forgot."

"We can do without the sarcasm," he said. "Wait a minute." He reached into her father's top desk drawer and extracted a bottle. "Come here."

She stopped with the width of the desk between them and held her hand out. He shook two capsules into her hand and recapped the bottle.

"Don't trust me with the whole bottle?" she taunted.

That was exactly how he felt, although he wasn't going to admit it. She'd had one too many upsets in the past few weeks. Normally as sound as a rock, even Tiffany could be pushed over the edge by grief and worry. He couldn't add the fear of bankruptcy to her store of problems. That one he could spare her. Let her think him a philanderer, if it helped. When she was strong enough, he'd tell her the truth.

"Take those and try to sleep," he said. "Things will look brighter in the morning."

She stared at the capsules with wounded wet eyes. "He was my rudder," she said in a husky whisper. "No matter how bad things got, he was always here to run to."

His face hardened. Once, he'd been there to run

to, before they married and became enemies. "You'll never know how sorry I am," he said tightly. "If you believe nothing else, believe that I didn't cause him to have that heart attack. I didn't argue with him over Carla."

She glanced at him and saw the pain in his eyes for the first time. It took most of the fight out of her. She seemed to slump. "I know you cared about my father, King," she said heavily.

"And in case you're wondering," he added with a mocking smile, "she's gone. She has her severance pay and some sort of reference. You won't see her again."

She studied him silently. "Why?"

"Why, what?"

"Why did my father fire her?"

It was like walking on eggshells, but he had to tell her the truth. "Because she dragged me home from Jamaica with a nonexistent emergency, just to interfere with our honeymoon, and he knew it. He said he'd had enough of her meddling."

"So had I," she returned.

"Not half as much as I had," he said curtly. "Harrison beat me to the punch by five minutes."

"He did?"

"Come here."

He looked faintly violent, and he'd been drinking. She hesitated.

He got up and came around the desk, watching her back away. "Oh, hell, no, you don't," he said in a voice like silk. His arms slid under her and he lifted her clear of the floor. "I've listened to you until I'm deaf. Now you can listen to me."

He went back to his chair and sat down with Tiffany cradled stiffly in his arms.

"No need to do your imitation of a plank," he chided, making himself comfortable. "Drunk men make bad lovers. I'm not in the mood, anyway. Now, you listen!"

She squirmed, but he held her still.

"Carla wasn't supposed to have anything to do with the flowers for our wedding," he said shortly. "I gave that task to Edna, who heads the personnel department, because she grew up in a florist's shop. But I was out of the office and Carla went to her with a forged letter that said I wanted Carla to do it instead."

Tiffany actually gasped.

He nodded curtly. "And she didn't get those arrangements from a florist, she did them herself with wilted flowers that she either got from a florist, or from a florist's trash can! She never had any intention of bringing you a bouquet, either. The whole thing was deliberate."

"How did you find out?"

"I went to see Edna when I flew back from Jamaica and found there was no emergency. I gave her hell about the flowers," he said. "She gave it back, with interest. Then she told me what had really happened. I was livid. I'd gone straight to my office to have it out with Carla when I found your father there."

"Oh."

He searched her stunned eyes. "You don't think much of me, do you?" he asked quietly. "Regardless of how I felt about the wedding, I wouldn't have deliberately hurt you like that."

She grimaced. "I should have known."

"You wore a suit to be married in," he added. "That was a blow to my pride. I thought you were telling me in a nonverbal way that you were just going through the motions."

"And I thought that you wouldn't mind what I wore, because you didn't want to marry me in the first place."

The arm behind her shoulders contracted, and the big, warm hand at the end of it smoothed over her upper arm in an absent, comforting motion. "I drew away from you at a time when we should have been talking about our insecurities," he said after a minute. "We had too many secrets. In fact, we still have them." He took a quick breath. "Tiffany, your father's personal accountant just did a flit with the majority of your inheritance. I'll bet that's what really set your father off, not Carla, although she helped. He was upset because he knew he'd have to tell you what had happened when you came home."

Tiffany's eyes widened. "You mean, Daddy was robbed?"

"In a nutshell," he agreed. He smiled faintly. "So, along with all your other woes, my wife, you may have bankruptcy looming unless I can find that accountant and prosecute him."

"I'm broke?" she said.

He nodded.

She sighed. "There goes my yacht."

"What do you want with one of those?"

She kept her eyes lowered demurely. Her heart was racing, because they were talking as they'd never talked before. "I thought I'd dangle it on the waterfront for bait and see if I could catch a nice man to marry."

That sounded like the girl he used to know. His eyes began to twinkle just faintly and he smiled. "What are you going to do with the husband you've already got?"

She studied his lean face with pursed lips. "I thought you were going to divorce me."

One eyebrow levered up. His eyes dropped to her slender body and traced it with arrogant possession. "Think again."

Chapter Ten

The look in his eyes was electric and Tiffany watched him watching her for long, exquisite seconds before his head began to bend.

She lay in his arms, waiting, barely breathing as he drew her closer. It seemed like forever since he'd kissed her, and she wanted him. She reached up, barely breathing, waiting...

The sudden intrusion of Lettie with a tray of coffee and cookies was as explosive as a bomb going off. They both jerked.

She hesitated just inside the door and stared at them. "Shall I go away?" she asked, chuckling.

King recovered with apparent ease. "Not if those are lemon cookies," he said.

Tiffany gasped, but he got up and helped her to her feet with a rakish grin. "Sorry, honey, but lemon cookies are my greatest weakness."

"Do tell," she murmured with her hands on her hips.

He gave her a thorough going-over with acquisitive eyes. "My *second* greatest weakness," he said, correcting her.

"Too late now," she told him and moved a little self-consciously toward Lettie as King swept forward and took the heavy tray from her.

He put it on the coffee table and they gathered around it while Lettie poured coffee into thin china cups and distributed saucers and cookies.

"I'm going to be poor, Lettie," Tiffany told Lettie.

"Not yet, you're not," King murmured as he savored a cookie. "I'll get in touch with the private detective your father hired to trail your elusive accountant, not to mention Interpol. He'll be caught."

"Poor Daddy," Tiffany sighed, tearing a little as she thought of her loss. "He must have only found out."

"About two days before the heart attack, I think," Lettie said heavily. She leaned over to pick up her coffee. "I tried to get him to see a doctor even then. His color wasn't good. That was unusual, too, because Harrison was always so robust—" She broke off, fighting tears.

Tiffany put an arm around her. "There, there," she said softly. "He wouldn't want us to carry on like this."

"No, he wouldn't," King added. "But we'll all grieve, just the same. He was a good man."

Tiffany struggled to get in a deep breath. She bit halfheartedly into a cookie and smiled. "These are good."

"There's a bakery downtown, where they make them fresh every day," Lettie confided.

"I know where it is," King mused. "I stop by there some afternoons to buy a couple to go with my coffee."

Tiffany glanced at him a little shyly and smiled. "I didn't know you liked cookies."

He looked back at her, but he didn't smile. "I didn't know you were allergic to aspirin."

He sounded as if not knowing that fact about her really bothered him, too.

"It's the only thing," she replied. She searched his drawn features. "King, you couldn't have known about Daddy's heart. I didn't even know. You heard what the doctor said. There was no history of heart trouble, either."

He stared at his half-eaten cookie. "It didn't help to have him upset..."

She touched his hand. "It would have happened anyway," she said, and she was sure of it now. "You can only control so much in life. There are always going to be things that you can't change."

He wouldn't meet her eyes. His jaw was drawn tight.

"Yes, I know, you don't like being out of control, in any way," she said gently, surprising him. "But neither of us could have prevented what happened. I remember reading about a politician who had a heart attack right in his doctor's office, and nobody could save him. Do you see what I mean?''

He reached out his free hand and linked it with hers. ''I suppose so.''

Lettie sipped coffee, lost in her own thoughts. She missed Harrison, too. The house was empty without him. She looked up suddenly. ''Good Lord, you only had a one-day honeymoon,'' she exclaimed.

''It was a good day,'' King murmured.

''Yes, it was,'' Tiffany said huskily, and his fingers contracted around hers.

''We'll finish it when we solve our problems here,'' King replied. ''We have all the time in the world.''

Tiffany nodded.

''It will be a shame if you can't catch that crook,'' Lettie said, looking around her at the beauty of the study. ''This house is the beginning of a legacy. Harrison had hoped to leave it to his grandchildren.''

Tiffany felt King stiffen beside her. Slowly, she unlinked her hand with his and put both hands around her coffee cup.

''We have years to talk about children,'' she told Lettie deliberately. ''Some couples don't ever have them.''

''Oh, but you will, dear,'' Lettie murmured dreamily. ''I remember how we used to go shopping, and the nursery department was always the first place you'd stop. You'd touch little gowns and booties and smile and talk about babies...''

Tiffany got to her feet, hoping her sudden paleness wouldn't upset Lettie. She had no way of knowing that King didn't want a child.

"I'm so tired, Lettie," she said, and looked it. She smiled apologetically. "I'd like to try to go back to sleep, if you don't mind."

"Of course not, dear. Can you sleep now, do you think?"

Tiffany reached into the pocket of her robe and produced the two capsules King had given her. She picked up her half-full cup of coffee and swallowed them. "I will now," she said as she replaced the cup in the saucer. "Thank you, King," she added without looking directly at him.

"Will you be all right?" he asked.

She felt that he was trying to make her look at him. She couldn't bear to, not yet. She was thinking about the long, lonely years ahead with no babies. She didn't dare hope that their only night together would produce fruit. That one lapse wasn't enough to build a dream on. Nobody got pregnant the first time. Well, some people did, but she didn't have that sort of luck. She wondered if King remembered how careless he'd been.

"I hope you both sleep well," she said as she went from the room.

"You, too, dear," Lettie called after her. She finished her coffee. "I'll take the tray back to the kitchen."

"I'll do it," King murmured. He got up and

picked it up, less rocky on his feet now that he'd filled himself full of caffeine.

"Are you going to try to sleep?"

He shook his head. "I've got too much work to do. It may be the middle of the night here, but I can still do business with half the world. I have to wrap up some loose ends. Tomorrow, I'm going to have my hands full tracing that accountant."

Lettie went with him to the kitchen and sorted out the things that needed washing.

King paused at the door, his face solemn and thoughtful. "Stay close to Tiffany tomorrow, will you?" he asked. "I don't want her alone."

"Of course, I will." She glanced at him. "Are you worried about Carla?"

He nodded. "She's always been high-strung, but just lately she seems off balance to me. I don't think she'd try to do anything to Tiffany. But there's no harm in taking precautions."

"I wish..." she began and stopped.

"Yes. I wish I'd never gotten involved with her, either," he replied, finishing the thought for her. "Hindsight is a grand thing."

"Indeed it is." She searched his bloodshot eyes. "You aren't sorry you married Tiffany?"

"I'm sorry I waited so long," he countered.

"But there are still problems?" she probed gently.

He drew in a long breath. "She wants babies and I don't."

"Oh, King!"

He winced. "I've been a bachelor all my life," he said shortly. "Marriage was hard enough. I haven't started adjusting to it yet. Fatherhood..." His broad shoulders rose and fell jerkily. "I can't cope with that. Not for a long time, if ever. It's something Tiffany will have to learn to live with."

Lettie bit down on harsh words. She sighed worriedly. "Tiffany's still very young, of course," she said pointedly.

"Young and full of dreams," King agreed. He stared at the sink. "Impossible dreams."

Outside the door, the object of their conversation turned and made her way slowly back upstairs, no longer thirsty for the glass of milk she'd come to take to bed with her. So there it was. King would never want a child. If she wanted him, it seemed that she'd have to give up any hopes of becoming a mother. Some women didn't want children. It was a pity that Tiffany did.

She didn't have to avoid King in the days that followed. He simply wasn't home. Business had become overwhelming in the wake of Harrison Blair's death. There were all sorts of legalities to deal with, and King had a new secretary who had to learn her job the hard way. He was very seldom home, and when he was, he seemed to stay on the telephone.

Lettie was still in residence, because Tiffany had begged her to stay. The house was big and empty without Harrison, but Lettie made it bearable. And on the rare occasions when King was home, their meals weren't silent ones. Lettie carried on conversations with herself if no one else participated, which amused Tiffany no end.

She hadn't paid much attention to the date. She'd grieved for two long weeks, crying every time she saw familiar things of her father's, adjusting to life without him. But just as she was getting used to the lonely house, another unexpected complication presented itself.

Tiffany suddenly started losing her breakfast. She'd never had any such problems before, and even if it was too soon for tests, deep inside she knew that she was pregnant. She went from boundless joy to stifling fear in a matter of seconds as she realized how this news was going to affect her husband. Her hands went protectively to her flat stomach and she groaned out loud.

She couldn't tell him. He wouldn't want the baby, and he might even suggest...alternatives. There wasn't an option she was willing to discuss. She was going to have her baby, even if she had to leave him and hide it away. That meant that she had to keep her condition secret.

At first it was easy. He was never home. But as the demands of business slowed a couple of weeks later, he began to come home earlier. And he was attentive, gentle with Tiffany, as if he were trying to undo their rocky beginning and start over.

It wounded her to the quick to have to withdraw from those sweet overtures, because she needed him now more than at any time in their shared past. But it was too great a risk to let him come close. Her body was changing. He wasn't stupid. If he saw her unclothed, there were little signs that even a bachelor might notice.

Her behavior surprised him, though, because they'd become much closer after Harrison's death. He'd had business demands that had kept him away from home, and he'd deliberately made very few demands on Tiffany just after her father's death, to give her time to adjust. But now, suddenly, she was talking about going back to modeling in New York, with Lettie to keep her company.

King worried about her attitude. He'd been kept busy with the transfer of authority and stocks and the implementation of Harrison's will, not to mention tracking down the elusive accountant. Perhaps she'd thought he wasn't interested in her feelings. That wasn't true. But when he tried to talk to her, she found dozens of excuses to get out of his vicinity.

Even Lettie was puzzled and remarked about Tiffany's coldness to the man, when he'd done so much for them. But Tiffany only smiled and ignored every word she said. Even from Lettie, the bouts of nausea were carefully concealed. No one was going to threaten her baby, Tiffany told herself. Not even Lettie, who might unwittingly let the cat out of the bag.

She talked about going to New York, but all the while, she was checking into possible escape routes. She could fly anywhere in the world that she wanted to go. Even without her father's fortune, she had a legacy from her mother, which guaranteed her a tidy fixed sum every month paid into her personal checking account. She could live quite well and take care of her child. All she needed was a place to go.

King found her one afternoon poring over travel brochures, which she gathered with untidy haste and stuffed back into a folder as if she'd been caught stealing.

"Planning a trip?" he asked, scowling as he stood over her.

She sat forward on the sofa. "Who, me? No!" She cleared her throat. "Well, not immediately, at least. I thought…" She hesitated while she tried to formulate an answer that would throw him off the track.

"Heard from your friend Mark?" he asked abruptly.

"Mark?" She'd all but forgotten her modeling friend, although she saw Lisa occasionally, and Lisa certainly heard from him. They were becoming an item. "I believe he's in Greece," she added. "Doing a commercial for some swimwear company."

"Yes, he is," King replied thoughtfully. "I saw Lisa's father at a civic-club meeting this week. He said that the two of them are quite serious."

"I'm glad," Tiffany said. "Mark's had a hard life. So has Lisa, in some ways. She's always had money, but her father is a very domineering sort. I hope he isn't planning to throw a stick into their spokes." ·

"Apparently Lisa's threatened to run away if he does," he mused, and smiled. "Love does make a woman brave, I suppose."

She could have made a nasty remark about Carla, but she let it go and made some careless remark.

"Don't you eat breakfast anymore?" he asked abruptly.

She jumped. "I... Well, no, I don't, really," she stammered. "I've gotten into bad habits since Daddy died," she added with a nervous laugh. "Breakfast reminds me too much of him."

"Which is still no reason to starve yourself, is it?"

She shifted, tracing a flower in the pattern on her skirt. "I'm not starving myself. I just don't like eating breakfast at the table. I have it in my room."

He stood there without speaking, frowning, jingling the loose change in his pocket.

She glanced at the clock and then at him. "Aren't you home early?" she asked.

"Yes." He moved to the armchair beside the sofa and dropped into it. "I thought you might like to know that we've found the runaway accountant."

"Have you really!"

He chuckled at her radiance. "Vengeful girl. Yes, he thought he'd gotten clean away. He was passing the time in luxurious splendor on a private island in the Bahamas when some rogue popped a bag over his head, trussed him up like a duck, and carted him off to a sailboat. He was hauled onto the beach in Miami and summarily arrested."

"Do we know rogues who would do such a thing?" she asked.

He chuckled. "Of course we do!"

"Does he still have any money?"

"All but a few thousand," he replied. "He confessed wholeheartedly when faced with a long prison term for his pains. He offered to give the money back without any prompting. To do him credit, he was sorry about Harrison."

"My father might still be here, if it hadn't been for that skunk. I won't shed any tears for him," she muttered. "I hope he isn't going to get off with a slap on the wrist."

"Not a chance," he replied. "He'll serve time. And he'll never get another job of trust."

"I suppose that's something. But it won't bring Daddy back."

"Nothing will do that."

She crossed her legs and glanced at King. He was restless and irritable. "What's wrong?" she asked.

"I wish I didn't have to tell you."

She sat up, bracing herself for anything. After what she'd just come through, she felt that she could take it on the chin, though, whatever it was. She was stronger than she'd ever been.

"Go ahead," she said. "Whatever it is, I can take it."

He looked at her, saw the new lines in her face, the new maturity. "How you've changed, Tiffany," he murmured absently.

"Stop stalling," she said.

He let out a hollow laugh. "Am I? Perhaps so." He leaned forward, resting his forearms across his knees. "I want you to see a doctor."

Her eyebrows arched. "Me? What for?"

"Because we're married," he replied evenly. "And I've gone without you for as long as I can. That being the case, you have to make some sort of preparation about birth control. We can't have any more lapses."

Steady, girl, she told herself. You can't give the show away now. She swallowed. "You said that you'd take care of it," she hedged.

"Yes, I did, didn't I?" he reflected with a laugh. "And you remember how efficiently I did it, don't you?" he asked pointedly.

She flushed. "It was…unexpected."

"And exquisite," he said quietly. "I dream about how it was. I've tried to wait, to give you time to get over the trauma of losing Harrison. But, to put it bluntly, I'm hurting. I want you."

She felt her cheeks go hot. She still wasn't sophisticated enough for this sort of blunt discussion. "All right," she said. "I'll see the doctor."

"Good girl." He got up and moved toward the sofa, reaching down to pull her up into his arms with a long sigh. "I miss you in my bed, Tiffany," he murmured as he bent to her mouth. "I want you so badly…!"

His mouth opened on hers and she moaned harshly at the pleasure of his embrace. She reached up and held him around the neck, pressing her body to his, moving provocatively, involuntarily.

He groaned harshly and his hands went to her waist to pull her closer. Then, suddenly, he stilled. Holding her rigidly, he lifted his head. His breath seemed to catch in his throat. His eyes looked straight into hers. And while she was trying to decide what had made him stop, his hands smoothed with deliberation over her thick waist and, slowly, down over the faint swell of her stomach.

His face changed. She knew the instant he began to suspect. It was all there, the tautness, the shock, the horror.

She jerked away from him, her face stiff with pain. The breath she drew was painful.

He let his arms fall to his sides. The look he sent to her belly would have won a photo contest.

"No, I won't." She choked out the words before he could speak. She backed toward the door. "I won't do anything about it, I don't care what you say, what you do! It's mine, and I'm going to have it! Do you hear me, I'm going to have it!"

She whirled and ran toward the staircase, desperate to reach the sanctuary of her room. She could lock the door and he couldn't get in, she could outrun him! But out of the corner of her eye, she saw him racing toward her. She'd never make the staircase, not at the speed he was running.

She turned at the last second and went toward the front door, panic in her movements, nausea in her throat. She jerked open the front door and forgot the rain that had made the brick porch as slick as glass. Her feet went out from under her and she fell with a horrible, sickening thud, right on her back.

"Tiffany!"

King's exclamation barely registered. She knew every bone in her body was broken. She couldn't even breathe, much less talk. She had the breath knocked completely out of her. She stared at his white face and didn't really see it at all.

"My...baby," she moaned with the only bit of breath she could muster.

King knelt beside her, his hands running over her gently, feeling for breaks while he strangled on every breath he took. There was a faint tremor in his long fingers.

"Don't try to move," he said uneasily. "Dear God...!" He got up and went back to the doorway. "Lettie! Lettie, get an ambulance, she's fallen!"

"Is she all right?" Lettie's wail came out the door.

"I don't know. Call an ambulance!"

"Yes, dear, right now...!"

King knelt beside Tiffany and took her cold, nerveless hand in his. The rain was coming down steadily beyond the porch, like a curtain between the two of them and the world.

Tiffany sucked in shallow breaths. Tears ran down her cheek. One hand lifted to her stomach. She began to sob. "My baby," she wept. "My baby!"

"Oh, God, don't!" he groaned. He touched her

wet cheeks with the backs of his fingers, trying to dry the tears. "You're all right, sweetheart, you're going to be fine. You're going to be fine...Lettie! For God's sake!"

Lettie came at a run, pausing at the slick porch. "I've phoned, and they're on the way right now." She moved onto the wet surface and looked down at Tiffany. "Oh, my dear," she groaned, "I'm so sorry!"

Tiffany was beyond words. She couldn't seem to stop crying. The tears upset King more than she'd ever seen anything upset him. He found his handkerchief and dried her wet eyes, murmuring to her, trying to comfort her.

She closed her eyes. She hurt all over, and she'd probably lost the baby. She'd never get another one. He'd make sure that she took precautions from now on, she'd grow old without the comfort of a child, without the joy of holding her baby in her arms...

The sobs shook her.

King eased down beside her, regardless of the wet floor, and his big hand flattened gently over her flat stomach, pressing tenderly.

"Try not to worry," he whispered at her lips. He kissed her softly, and his hand moved protectively. "The baby's all right. I know he is."

Chapter Eleven

Tiffany couldn't believe what she'd just heard. Her eyes opened and looked straight into his.

"You don't want it," she whispered.

He drew in a rough breath and his hand spread even more. "Yes, I do," he said quietly. "I want both of you."

She could barely get enough breath to speak, and before she could find the words, the ambulance drowned out even her thoughts as it roared up at the front steps and two EMTs disembarked.

She was examined and then put into the ambulance. King went with her, promising Lettie that he'd phone the minute he knew anything.

Tiffany felt him grasp her hand as the ambulance started up again. "You're forever taking me away in ambulances," she whispered breathlessly.

He brought her hand to his mouth and kissed the

palm hungrily. "Wherever you go, I go, Tiffany," he said. But his eyes were saying other things, impossible things. They took the rest of her breath away.

She was taken to the local emergency room and checked thoroughly, by the family physician who was doing rounds.

Dr. Briggs chuckled at her when he'd finished his tests and had the results, over an hour later. "I heard about your wild ride in Montego Bay. Now, here you are in a fall. Maybe marriage doesn't agree with you," he teased, having known her from childhood.

"It agrees with her," King murmured contentedly, watching her with open fascination. "So will having a baby to nurse." He glanced at Briggs. "Is she?"

He nodded, smiling complacently at Tiffany's gasp and radiant smile. "I don't imagine we'll have much trouble computing a delivery date," he added wickedly.

Tiffany flushed and King chuckled.

"One time," he murmured dryly. "And look what you did," he accused.

"What I did!" she exclaimed.

"I only plant. I don't cultivate."

She burst out laughing. She couldn't believe what she was hearing. All that talk about not wanting babies, and here he sat grinning like a Cheshire cat.

"He'll strut for a while," the doctor told her. "Then he'll start worrying, and he won't do any more strutting until after the delivery. You'll have to reassure him at frequent intervals. Expectant fathers," he said on a sigh, "are very fragile people."

"She'll have to have an obstetrician," King was murmuring aloud. He glanced at Briggs. "No offense."

"None taken," the doctor mused.

"A good obstetrician."

"I don't refer pregnant women to any other kind," he was assured.

"We'll need to find a good college, too..."

Tiffany started to protest, but King was at the window, talking to himself and Dr. Briggs held up a hand.

"Don't interrupt him," he told Tiffany. "He's considering all the other appropriate families in town who have baby daughters. He'll have to have the right wife..."

"It could be a girl," she interjected.

"Heresy!" the doctor said in mock alarm.

"Shouldn't we point that out?" she continued, glancing at King.

Dr. Briggs shook his head. "A man has to have dynastic dreams from time to time." He smiled. "You're fine, Tiffany. A few bruises, but nothing broken and that baby is firmly implanted. Just don't overdo during the first trimester. Call me Monday and I'll refer you to an obstetrician. I do not," he added, "deliver babies. I like sleeping at night."

"Are babies born at night?"

"From what I hear, almost all of them," he said with a chuckle.

King took her home, still reeling with his discoveries. He carried her inside, cradling her like a treasure.

Lettie met them at the door, wringing her hands. "You didn't phone," she said accusingly.

"He was too busy arranging the wedding," Tiffany replied.

Lettie looked blank. "Wedding?"

"Our son's."

"Son." Lettie still looked blank. Then her face flushed with glorious surprise. "You're pregnant!"

"Yes," she said.

Lettie gnawed her lip and shot a worried glance at King.

"I know," he said wearily. "I'll have to eat boiled crow for the next month, and I deserve to." He shrugged, holding Tiffany closer. "I didn't know how it was going to feel," he said in his own defense, and he smiled with such tenderness that electricity seemed to run through her relaxed body. "What an incredible sensation."

Tiffany smiled and laid her cheek against his shoulder. "I'm sleepy," she said, yawning.

King glanced at Lettie. "I'm going to put her to bed."

"That's the best place for her," Lettie said with a warm smile. "Let me know if you need anything, dear," she told Tiffany, and bent to kiss the flushed cheek.

"I'll be fine. Thank you, Lettie."

King was grinning from ear to ear all the way up

the staircase, and he never seemed to feel her weight at all, because he wasn't even breathing hard by the time they reached the top.

"You don't want children," she murmured drowsily. "You said so."

"We're all entitled to one stupid mistake." He carried her to his room, not hers, and laid her gently on the coverlet. His eyes were solemn as he looked down at her. "For what it's worth, I do want this child. I want it very much. Almost as much as I want you."

She flushed. "King, Dr. Briggs said..." she began cautiously.

He put a finger over her lips. "He said that the first trimester is tricky," he replied. He nodded. "We won't make love again until the baby is at home." He bent and kissed her with aching tenderness. "But we'll sleep in each other's arms, as we should have been doing from the first night, when you were a virgin bride—a beautiful princess bride. If you're cold, I'll warm you. If you're afraid, I'll cuddle you." He pushed back her soft hair. His eyes looked deeply, hungrily into hers. "And if you want to be loved, I'll love you. Like this." His lips drew softly against her mouth, cherishing, tasting. His cheek rested on hers and he sighed. "I'll love you with all my heart," he whispered a little roughly. "For all my life."

Her caught breath was audible. "You...love me?"

"As much as you love me," he agreed. He lifted

his head and searched her eyes. "Didn't you think I knew?"

She sighed. "No. Not really."

"That's the only thing I was ever sure of, with you. And sometimes, I wondered why you loved me. I've been a lot of trouble. Still want to keep me, in spite of everything?"

She smiled slowly. "More than ever. Somebody has to teach the baby how to take over corporations when he or she is old enough."

He chuckled. "Well, you're stuck with me, whether you want me or not." He touched her cheek and looked at her with pale eyes that mirrored his awe and delight. "I never dreamed that it would feel like this to belong to someone, to have someone who belonged to me." He sighed. "I didn't think I could."

"I know why," she replied, tracing his mouth with her fingertip. "But we're not like your parents, King. We won't have their problems. We'll have each other and our child."

He began to smile. "So we will."

She drew him down to her lips and kissed him with pure possession. "Now, try to get away," she challenged under her breath.

He chuckled as he met her lips with his. "That works both ways."

She thought what a wonderful godmother Lettie would be to the new arrival, and how proud her father would have been. It made her a little sad to think of him.

But then her husband's warm, strong arms tightened gently around her and reminded her that in life, for each pain, there is a pleasure. She closed her eyes and her thoughts turned to lullabies as the rain beat softly on the roof.

* * * * *

In April, watch for
Diana Palmer's wonderful new story
THE BRIDE WHO WAS STOLEN IN THE NIGHT.
It is part of a new Silhouette Books Collection—
MONTANA MAVERICKS WEDDINGS!

DIANA PALMER
ANN MAJOR
SUSAN MALLERY

In **April 1998** get ready to catch the bouquet. Join in the excitement as these bestselling authors lead us down the aisle with three heartwarming tales of love and matrimony in Big Sky country.

RETURN TO WHITEHORN

A very engaged lady is having second thoughts about her intended; a pregnant librarian is wooed by the town bad boy; a cowgirl meets up with her first love. Which Maverick will be the next one to get hitched?

Available in **April 1998**.

Silhouette's beloved **MONTANA MAVERICKS** returns in Special Edition and Harlequin Historicals starting in February 1998, with brand-new stories from your favorite authors.

Round up these great new stories at your favorite retail outlet.

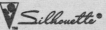

Look us up on-line at: http://www.romance.net

PSMMWEDS

Take 4 bestselling love stories FREE

a FREE surprise gift!

Special Limited-time Offer

Mail to Silhouette Reader Service®

P.O. Box 609
Fort Erie, Ontario
L2A 5X3

YES! Please send me 4 free Silhouette Romance™ novels and my free surprise gift. Then send me 6 brand-new novels every month, which I will receive months before they appear in bookstores. Bill me at the low price of $3.25 each plus 25¢ delivery and GST*. That's the complete price and a savings of over 10% off the cover prices—quite a bargain! I understand that accepting the books and gift places me under no obligation ever to buy any books. I can always return a shipment and cancel at any time. Even if I never buy another book from Silhouette, the 4 free books and the surprise gift are mine to keep forever.

315 SEN CF2Q

Name	(PLEASE PRINT)
Address	Apt. No.
City	Province Postal Code

This offer is limited to one order per household and not valid to present Silhouette Romance™ subscribers. *Terms and prices are subject to change without notice. Canadian residents will be charged applicable provincial taxes and GST.

CSROM-696   ©1990 Harlequin Enterprises Limited

ALICIA SCOTT

**Continues the
twelve-book series—
36 Hours—in March 1998
with Book Nine**

PARTNERS IN CRIME

The storm was over, and Detective Jack Stryker finally had a
prime suspect in Grand Springs' high-profile murder case. But
beautiful Josie Reynolds wasn't about to admit to the crime—
nor did Jack want her to. He believed in her innocence, and he
teamed up with the alluring suspect to prove it. But was he
playing it by the book—or merely blinded by love?

For Jack and Josie and *all* the residents of Grand Springs,
Colorado, the storm-induced blackout was just the beginning of
36 Hours that changed *everything!* You won't want to miss a
single book.

Available at your favorite retail outlet.

Return to the Towers!

In March
New York Times bestselling author

NORA ROBERTS

brings us to the Calhouns' fabulous
Maine coast mansion and reveals the
tragic secrets hidden there for generations.

For all his degrees, Professor Max Quartermain has a
lot to learn about love—and luscious Lilah Calhoun is
just the woman to teach him. Ex-cop Holt Bradford is
as prickly as a thornbush—until Suzanna Calhoun's
special touch makes love blossom in his heart.
And all of them are caught in the race to solve
the generations-old mystery of a priceless
lost necklace…and a timeless love.

Lilah and Suzanna THE Calhoun Women

**A special 2-in-1 edition containing
FOR THE LOVE OF LILAH and
SUZANNA'S SURRENDER**

Available at your favorite retail outlet.